Compass of Fates

Tales of the Overworld

Jules Pendragon

Compass of Fates

Tales of the Overworld

Jules Pendragon

First published in 2024 by Julieta Pereyra

Cover illustration © Alexandria McAlpine
Chapters illustrations © Canva

A catalogue of this book is available from the British Library.

ISBN 978-1-06-867422-8 (paperback)
ISBN 978-1-06-867423-5 (ebook)

Typeset in 11 / 13 pt. Adobe Caslon Pro by Julieta Pereyra
Editorial and Design by Julieta Pereyra

To those who are applying for jobs: you don't need a CV to work in the Overworld.

Foreword

Dear reader,

The process of bringing a book to life involves the hard work and dedication of many talented individuals. I am honoured to acknowledge the contributions of those who have played a crucial role in the production of this book.

My deepest gratitude goes to my talented designer Alexandria McAlpine, for creating a captivating cover that represents the true essence of this book.

A special thank you to Claire Baldwin, who helped me shape my style guide. Your expertise has been extremely essential throughout the editing process.

To Jessica Dunn, your advice during the eBook process was invaluable. Thank you for ensuring everything ran smoothly.

To Georgia Henley, Holly McLaughlin and Rose Taylor. Thank you for giving me the creative tools to promote this book.

I would also like to express my appreciation to my proofreader, Reyna Cox, and my typesetting advisors, Imogen Crockford and Kara Daniel. Thank you for your diligence in ensuring the manuscript was error free and polished to perfection.

And last but not least, thank you, Emma Tait, for your unwavering guidance as my supervisor for my Publishing Project. Thank you for providing me with your knowledge and encouragement throughout the entire process.

With all my love,

Julieta Pereyra
Managing Editor

TABLE OF CONTENTS

Pursuit 1

Flowers 19

Roadkill 35

Senses 53

Gathering 57

Falling 73

Dispute 109

Recollection 127

Acknowledgements 147

About the Author 151

PURSUIT

The moon hung high in the night sky, casting an ethereal glow over the empty streets of London. Silence blanketed the city, broken only by the distant echoes of muffled and purposeful footsteps.

A man darted through deserted and narrow alleyways. Desperation fuelled his frantic run, echoing the sound of ragged breaths and echoing footsteps. But no matter how hard he tried to elude his pursuer, he heard the footsteps of that shadowed figure even closer.

How had things come to this? What had he done to deserve such fate? His memories were glass shards, scattered across a foggy landscape. He remembered flashes of his past life – a life filled with ambition, desire and a thirst for success. He attended prestigious private institutions, where he excelled as the best in class. Armed with charisma and a razor-sharp wit, he climbed the ranks of the corporate world, leaving behind jealous colleagues in his wake.

He had been a young entrepreneur, driven by the relentless pursuit of wealth. His rise to power was swift and ruthless. He founded his own company, a startup born from a brilliant idea and an unwavering belief in his own abilities. Willing to take risks, he transformed his vision into reality, building an empire from the ground up. Endless meetings and deals during the day, and lavish parties and extravagant indulgencies during the night.

But amidst the glitz, there was darkness lurking beneath the surface. He had stepped on toes, betrayed trust and sacrificed his morals in the ruthless game of the corporate world. He had betrayed, yes, but he was fortunate enough that those deeds were forgiven and forgotten by the upper society.

His personal life suffered as well. Relationships crumbled beneath the weight of his ambitions; his family and friends were pushed aside in favour of business dealings. He became isolated, success being his sole companion – a sprawling penthouse overlooking the city skyline, luxury cars and designer suits.

In the final moments of his life, the man was ensnared in the throes of a lavish party, a glittering affair held in the opulent confines of his own property. The air was thick with the scent of expensive perfumes, and the sound of laughter mingled with the pulsating beat of techno music. They were celebrating a closed deal, in which he had to fire one of his most trusted seniors of the company. But it was of no consequence. This was, after all, the way capitalism worked. As the night wore on, the party reached its zenith. Guests adorned in designer attire sipped champagne and danced with abandon.

Fuelled by a potent cocktail of drugs and alcohol, he drifted further into a haze of euphoria and oblivion. He had been drawn to the allure of these temporary highs that these substances provided. But on this night, he had gone too far. In his intoxicated state, he teetered on the edge of the balcony, the city lights twinkling far below. He loved heights, the rush of adrenaline that came with standing on the precipice of danger. Which is why he never bothered with securing his balcony. As he leaned too far over the edge, he lost his footing, sending him tumbling into the abyss below. Time seemed to slow as he plummeted through the air, thirty floors down, his heart pounding in his chest as he braced for impact.

Darkness closed in around him.

An echoing, sickening thud.

And then, nothing.

The man recalled his first few moments after the fall. How he had looked around disoriented.

'Richard Miller,' a voice had snapped him out of his thoughts.

And that was when he saw *him*.

A tall figure hidden beneath a cloak of darkness walking towards him with eerie grace. There was nothing particular about him. He could be a business partner for all he knew. But there was something about his presence which made Richard's body go cold.

'I have come to collect you.'

At first, he thought it was a dream, then a joke. But when the truth sank in, he could not help but try to get out of it. After all, is that not how the world works?

'Look, man, I've got money, properties, cars, you name it,' Richard had bargained to the figure at one point during the conversation. 'Can we settle this and, you know, bring me back to life?'

'You cannot buy your way out of death,' the figure had replied. 'You are done here.'

The figure took out an object from his inner pocket. A golden hourglass. The sand had already reached the bottom, and the device shone, even in the dark.

That was when he felt a pull towards the hourglass. He looked down at his right arm, only to find it gone. Richard stumbled back. 'What the fuck? What is happening?!'

Richard had not waited for what the figure had to say. Instead, he had bolted down the building's front walkway and into the night. In the winding maze of the city's labyrinthine streets, Richard's strength waned. His breath came in ragged gasps, his legs trembling with fatigue as he made his way into a drenched alley. He glanced back over his shoulder and saw the figure closing in. He forced his legs to keep moving, desperate to escape.

Before he could take another step, the figure vanished from sight. In an instant, it reappeared directly in front of him, blocking his path. Richard barely had time to register the suddenness of the figure's appearance before a powerful fist struck him square in the left cheek. The force of the blow sent him sprawling to the wet ground, the air driven from his lungs in a painful gasp. Richard lay there, struggling to concentrate, as the figure loomed over him.

'You just bought a one-way ticket to the Netherworld,' he growled, his voice a chilling breeze that sent shivers through his spine.

Richard gazed up at the reaper, trembling. 'Please, spare me...'

'Spare you?' The figure raised his eyebrow. 'You're dead. I can't kill you, but I can certainly try if you'd like. Especially after you made me run half a mile. Do you know what would've happened had I not caught you? Extensive paperwork does not even begin to cover it.'

He took a step forward. 'As for you... You would've gone insane. See, dead souls have no purpose here. They're not welcome. Neither are they in the Overworld, since it's the bridge between the human world and the Afterlife. Instead, you would've become an errant spirit, and most of them look like the zombies you see in *The Walking Dead*. Some are more eloquent, yes, but the rest are just nasty. Believe me, I saved the last part of your wretched existence.

'Let's do this again, shall we? Richard Miller, born on the thirtieth of April 1989, aged four-and-thirty. I've come to collect you. I'll make sure your soul ends up where it belongs. And by the looks of it, it won't be anywhere good.'

'N-no, please!' Richard begged.

But what could he do? The cloaked man took that cursed hourglass again. And once more, his body shimmered to sand and felt himself being sucked into the device.

That guy was a dick.

Or so the reaper thought as he dragged his feet back to the Overworld. His legs felt like stone, but he was in no rush. There was still time before dawn. He recalled the chase and let out a grunt, scratching the bridge of his nose. Should he feel pity for him? Miller most likely did not understand half of the things he had said.

No matter.

After walking through Bishopsgate, he passed Liverpool Street and headed all the way down to the Tower of London. He stepped down to the pier, and once his foot dipped in the water, he found himself in the Judgement Room. The reaper wished they would redecorate. The crimson walls were too old for his taste – Baroque, an epoch he had lived but had stopped appreciating after witnessing the styles that succeeded it.

His feet itched to leave this place straight away. So many sinful souls were locked in this place, along with other unmentionable creatures, as part of the punishment they had to endure.

As if on cue, a limping figure walked towards him. The reaper's back straightened when he sensed its approach. 'It's been a while since you stepped into these halls, Mr. Reaper.'

'Samuel,' the reaper said, irritation flooding his words at the sight of the soul. 'It is always a pleasure to know that you are still dead. Tell me, does it hurt when they dip your face in boiling water?'

'With time, you get used to it.'

'Ah, your brain hasn't melted yet. You know how to answer. Anyway…' the reaper produced a silk pouch from the inner pocket of his coat. 'I'm here with a delivery.'

'You? One would assign other lesser reapers after gaining rank.'

'I decided to give my assistant a break. But I don't have time to entertain you with a chat. My schedule's packed. Lead the way.'

Samuel bowed at him, gritting its teeth, and limped through the hallway. Eager to get this done, the reaper adjusted his black coat and trailed behind the tortured soul. He wrinkled his nose. He had not gotten used to the stench of blood and flesh from this place. He also could not understand why reapers had to walk through this place, of all places, instead of having a shortcut built up. Were perhaps the Fates trying to remind them of the consequences if they didn't carry out their job? It was not as if they could ask them. Reapers only obeyed orders from above, not even knowing what the hell that was.

'Watch your step, Mr Reaper.' Samuel's voice snapped him out of his thoughts. The hallway led them to a narrow, straight pathway of stones that stretched all the way to an arch of five different doors. Make the wrong step, and one would find themselves falling into the chasm. Reapers were not stupid enough to jump, as they never knew where that abyss would lead them to. In a loop of nothingness, perhaps.

The reaper took confident strides, one step after the other. *Fucking redecorate*, he thought once more. This place was too humid to his liking. Once they landed to safety, he was guided to the third door, which creaked as it opened.

He knew Samuel could not enter beyond this point. Otherwise, the rest of its soul would be sucked out of it. The reaper walked straight past Samuel, not bothering to acknowledge it. He heard the door slam behind him.

'Welcome, Reaper,' a voice croaked through the dark room. Green-flamed torches lit at his arrival. When he had come here after some redecoration fifty years ago, he could not help but think that the torches were meant to simulate an antique stoplight. He would have made that remark were it not for the old lady in front of him that tended to greet him with those creepy yellow teeth of hers. She was indeed old, older than the creation of Earth. And it fucking looked like it.

With all the politeness he could muster, the reaper bowed at the crone sitting on the stoned throne. 'Ma'am, as usual, it's a pleasure to see you.'

'Liar,' she replied. 'I see right through you.'

Well then, the reaper's jaw clenched. *Enough with the pleasantries.* 'I'm here with a delivery.'

'And where is your handsome assistant? He always comes here with a bounty of—' *Yes, yes, he knew.*

'Away, Ma'am,' the reaper interrupted. And that, technically, was not a lie. 'I'm here in his stead. I may not bring as many souls tonight, but they will surely keep you entertained for a while.'

'Is that so?'

'Had to chase one of these today.' The reaper held out the pouch. 'In fact, I would love to see where that one in particular will end up in.'

'Ah, did it make you mad?'

'No, I'm just bored. Besides, it's been a while since I watched a trial. I'll even take notes like a good old student.'

'Do what you want,' the crone waved him off. 'Just don't stand in the way.'

His head bowed in thanks. He placed the hourglasses on the stoned table in front of them. There were a total of eight. He stepped away from the dais and headed to one of the corners of the hall. His back rested against the wall. Yes, it had been a while since he's been here. One would call him morbid from watching. But what did he care? He was dead. His soul had been judged. He was stuck here for all eternity.

'Which one bothered you?' the old lady asked.

The reaper stared at the hourglasses and pointed at the culprit. 'Richard Miller.'

The hourglass answered to his call, lifting off the stone and levitating a few inches away. The sand poured out of the device, a shape forming upwards until Miller materialised in the hallway. He stumbled a few steps forward and looked around as if he were going through a nightmare. He would not be wrong if this thought had crossed his feeble mind.

'Richard Miller, born on the thirtieth of April 1989, aged four-and-thirty,' the old lady called out. 'You hereby stand by your trial. Your soul will be judged fairly according to Article Six, Section two, Addendum B of the Overworld Codex.'

The reaper almost felt pity for the crone as she repeated the same thing all over again, day and night. Almost. He glanced at Miller, who was looking at the room, not knowing where he was, like every other soul that arrived at the Judgement Room. No one knew exactly what was happening until the very end. Souls shuffled through this room like cattle through a gate, each facing their own reckoning. Some bore the weight of their deeds upon their shoulders, while others remained ignorant until the last moment. Among the latter, many started with denial, followed by a bit of desperation and begging. Some were bold enough to face it with a straight face. Those were the ones who had acknowledged that there was indeed something was out there waiting for them. But what he detested with all his might were the ones called 'believers'. What, did they think that praying would grant them paradise without doing good deeds? Now those he enjoyed watching.

'Place your hourglass on the scale,' the crone ordered.

Miller was sensible enough to obey. He grabbed the floating hourglass and walked a few steps towards the dais, where the silver scale was situated. A crow's feather had been placed on one side of the scale.

'Let the records of Richard Miller's life be presented for judgement.' The crone continued her solemn recitation, her voice a monotone drone that filled the chamber.

As the hourglass settled into place, the scales tipped, the feather outweighing the sands of time. The reaper felt no joy in Miller's fate, no satisfaction in his downfall. It was simply the way of things, the natural order of existence. In the end, all souls must face their reckoning, whether they be saints or sinners, believers or sceptics.

'Please, I beg of you! Show mercy!' Miller's voice cracked with desperation as he fell to his knees, his eyes wide.

The crone's expression remained unchanged as she regarded the pleading soul before her. 'Your fate has been decided, Richard Miller. No amount of begging will alter it. You have been sentenced to forty-two years in the Netherworld's Punishment Chamber, which represents the number of lives you have ruined multiplied by seven.'

With a wave of her gnarled hand, Miller was engulfed in a swirling vortex of shadows, his cries echoing through the chamber as he was whisked away.

The portal closed behind him. The reaper remained silent, knowing he was merely an observer in this cosmic drama. It was not his place to intervene. He was but a harbinger of the inevitable, a witness to the eternal dance of life and death. In the Netherworld, there are no second chances, no redemption for those who have strayed from the path of righteousness.

After that forty-two-year punishment, Miller would be condemned to spend the rest of his time in the Limbo Circle, his memories being sucked by wraiths until his time of reincarnation arrived. And who knew when that was going to be?

'Satisfied?' the crone turned to the reaper.

Suddenly, the pebbles on the floor were much more interesting. 'Not my place to comment, Ma'am.'

'But if you had a say?'

The reaper let out an inaudible sigh before turning towards the old lady. He had the reasonable desire to leave this wretched place. 'Cases like this make me wonder how fair these trials are, really. Miller cheated on his wife, that's one. He got two of his so called best friends addicted to MDMA, going up to three. He fired his best partner in the middle of a cost-of-living crisis, four. He committed a hit-and-run on a passerby, while intoxicated, and no one caught him, five. And he refused to acknowledge that he had a son, six. And yet each of these lives is worth of seven years? Sounds pretty bullshit to me. And I wonder how this person got forty-two years, but another can get more than two hundred.'

The crone straightened up her back despite her hunchback and narrowed her eyes at him. 'His soul was judged according to the damage he made to them.'

'He scarred them for life,' the reaper complained and noticed he had raised his voice too much to his superior. He cleared his throat and bowed his head to the crone. 'I think I've seen enough for today.'

The reaper pivoted and headed to the door, wanting to remove himself from this place right this instant. He did not even want to witness the rest of the collected souls anymore.

'Your wife maimed and killed six souls, boy!' the crone's voice echoes in the room. 'The punishment had to be harder.'

The reaper clenched his jaw, but his steps did not falter on his way out. Things could go south for him if he stood up to her.

The sun was rising by the time he left the Judgement Room. The skies turned shades of orange and pink above the Southbank path. He found an empty bench to stare at the river. He enjoyed the quietness of the morning and the lack of rain, which occurred most days. His tranquil break did not last long, however, as a figure dressed in as much as black as he was sat next to him. The newcomer held out a cup and the reaper could smell the strong coffee in it. He grabbed it without much thought.

'Thanks,' he mumbled before taking a sip. 'Did you do what I asked?'

The assistant nodded. 'I found the girl.'

'Good, keep her hourglass well hidden. I'll tell you when I'll collect it.' The reaper could trust that his colleague would do the job well.

Only thirty days remained until he saw her again. He trusted she would excel in the Dream Exam – the entrance to become a reaper, like them.

'Yes, sir,' the assistant leaned back on the bench and took a sip of his own plastic cup. 'Rough night, huh?'

The reaper shrugged. It was best to leave it that way. Not every soul's journey is worth being told. 'In this world, every night is a rough night. You either get used to it or—'

'Quit?' the reaper's assistant supplied.

'You never quit.'

'You could quit, you know. Everyone does at one point. I heard Beanie will hand her resignation after collecting her millionth soul.'

But the reaper could collect ten million souls, and yet it wouldn't be enough. 'Then there wouldn't be justice.'

'Yeah… I know,' the assistant nodded, his understanding implicit. With a brief glance at the hourglass in his grasp, he shifted his attention to his superior. 'So, are you up for a rough day?'

The reaper paused, taking a deliberate sip of his coffee before addressing his colleague. Retrieving the hourglass from the assistant's hand, he examined it, as if he could look into the soul's past life within its sands.

'Who's next?'

FLOWERS

Humans are inaccurate with their facts. One cannot fault them. To this day, half of them believe the Earth is flat, whereas the other half claim Earth is the centre of the universe. We are currently placing our hopes on Nicolaus Copernicus. It is unfortunate that he will die so soon after speaking his truth.

As for religion, humans do not know who to worship, and bloodshed is not uncommon when done in the name of one they would only call 'God'. It is ironic. Don't their texts have a passage on how ending the life of another is a sin? And yet they end lives only for not believing in the same religion as them.

Not even in death does one truly find out the truth. Humans are a minuscule part of the vast cosmos. They are not as superior as they think they are. So inessential that they do not deserve to know. Reapers, on the other hand, learn about the necessary fragments of the whole. Only what is necessary to complete their tasks.

It all began with the God of the Darkness and the Goddess of the Night. We are not allowed to know their names. Names are too powerful. We know that they have ruled over the dead ever since mankind was created. Their offspring, the Fates, were in charge of creating the souls and determining their life spans, whereas the godly pair would lead them to the Afterlife.

But mankind expanded. Perhaps too much. That was when they realised that five entities were not enough. One of the Fates, Future, sought an audience with the gods and proposed the creation of the *torva messor*.

The cold hand of death.

The reaper.

They would be handpicked humans between the mortal ages of eighteen and thirty that would have died that same year. The *torva messor* would be bestowed with powers beyond mortal comprehension, tasked with shepherding souls from the realm of the living to the realm of the dead. Their eyes would hold the weight of eternity, their touch the chill of the grave. They would walk the fine line between worlds, unseen yet ever present, fulfilling their grim purpose with a solemnity born of ages past.

The Goddess of Nature opposed. She argued that meddling with the delicate balance between life and death would bring unforeseen consequences, upsetting the harmony that she had meticulously woven into the fabric of existence. But her pleas fell upon deaf ears as the other gods, intoxicated by their own ambition, turned a blind eye to her warnings. And so, against the protests of Nature, the *torva messor* were created, their existence a testament to the hubris of divine beings.

It was an experiment, and errors were expected. First came the *coloratus*. The coloured eyed. The saint. The memory bringer. Tasked with guiding souls with compassion and grace to their final destination in the great beyond. The *coloratus* possessed a rare and wondrous gift – the ability to crystallise the memories of mortals. With a touch as delicate as a whisper, they could coax forth shimmering gems from the depths of a mortal's mind, each crystal a testament to a life once lived, a story once told.

But the Fates' blessings did not end there. In recognition of the *coloratus's* sacred duty, they bestowed upon them a relic of profound significance: an hourglass. Its glass was smooth and unblemished, its sands an unending cascade of time itself, its frame gold as the light of dawn. Within its confines lay the power to both measure the passage of mortal lives and house the souls of the departed, a solemn duty entrusted solely to the saint.

Yet, for all their gifts and responsibilities, the *coloratus* remained bound by the immutable laws of existence. Try as they might, they could not replicate the hourglass nor conjure another like it. It became apparent to the gods that the *coloratus* needed balance, a counterpart to temper their mercy with judgement. Thus came the *argenteum*. The silver eyed. The sinner. The truth revealer. Void of memories, but full of wisdom and impartiality. Together, the saint and the sinner formed a symbiotic union, their contrasting essences weaving together to fulfil the sacred purpose for which they were created.

The saint and the sinner needed a place to live, train, and teach the newly anointed reapers. And so, the Goddess of the Night and the God of the Underworld created a land for them – a bridge between the Afterlife and the human world called the Overworld. This realm was neither bound by time nor fully detached from it; a liminal space, where the air was thick with an ethereal mist and in its heart stood the magnificent academy made of sand coloured marble.

Academiae Fatorum.

The Academy of Fates.

To this day, its architecture astounds me. A seamless blend of ancient majesty and ethereal grace. Every time I look at the luminescent stone that forms its structure, changing hues with the time of day, I feel a deep sense of awe. The runic symbols that adorn the exterior make me feel like I am part of something much greater.

Walking through the vast archway at the entrance, crowned with its celestial map, I feel a shiver of excitement. The Grand Atrium is my favourite spot to pause and admire. Its polished obsidian floor mirrors the sky above, creating a breathtaking illusion. The towering columns surrounding the atrium, inscribed with the names of legendary reapers, make me feel connected to a long lineage of guardians. I often find myself tracing the names with my fingers, wondering about their lives and stories.

But it is the Hall of Echoes that truly captures my heart. This circular chamber, with its walls pulsing with a faint, rhythmic glow, is a place of deep reflection. We gather here to listen to the voices of the past, of those wise guides that came before us. The mosaic in the ceiling depicts the endless cycle of life, death and rebirth. Each visit reminds me of why we do what we do.

I cherish the time spent on the training grounds. I love running through the open fields of silver grass and stoned bridges. The dense forests and serene lakes provide peaceful retreats for meditation, where I can connect deeply with the essence of magick that flows through the Overworld.

The Library of Eternities is another sanctuary for me. This vast labyrinthine structure, lined with ancient tomes and scrolls, is a treasure trove of knowledge. The crisp air filled with the faint scent of parchment and ink makes it a perfect place for deep study. I immerse myself in these texts, some even belonging to departed souls, whose manuscripts have been unpublished.

The Sanctum of Memories is where the saints impart their wisdom, and it's one of the most moving places in the academy. Or so I believe, as I cannot help but be subjective about this place. Filled with soft light and preserved memories, this place feels sacred. Crystalline structures, each containing a fragment of mortal life, fill the room with a soft rainbow glow. Here, I learn to appreciate the fragility of human existence, understanding the care required in handling the souls we guide.

And last but not least, despite that I do not find myself here as often as I would like, I cannot help but mention the Chamber of Sands. Here, the sinners create hourglasses of sand, each one representing a mortal soul. The room is filled with shelves upon shelves of these hourglasses. It hums with the ticking of countless grains of sand, a constant reminder of the rapid passage of time. Watching the sinners work is mesmerising as they handle each hourglass with precision.

I often stand in the shadows, observing my partner, Reaper Tatius, as he crafts these hourglasses. Tatius's focus is unwavering, his movements deliberate. He selects the sands with a discerning eye, knowing that each grain must be perfect. The hourglasses themselves are works of art if you ask me.

I hope I am not boring you with details of what you already know. However, despite existing in the Overworld for over five hundred years, I remain feeling fortuitous and honoured to be in this very moment. Not many are graced with the opportunity to stand in this realm as we are.

And yes, the construction of the academy marked the beginning of a new era – a testament to the gods' determination to maintain the balance between life and death. The legacy of the *torva messor* still continues. Every hundred years, amidst the celestial dance of the stars and the blood moon, a new generation of reapers is chosen to bear the mantle of our sacred duty. One that begins with the Dream Exam. A test of both mind and spirit. I have witnessed this sacred ritual unfold a couple of times during my time here.

The candidates, drawn from their dreams, gather in the Dream Realm of the Overworld, their souls laid bare before the luminous glow of the moon. Some are confronted with visions of their past deeds, forced to confront the consequences of their actions. Others are tested by treacherous landscapes and riddles that probe the depths of their intellect.

As the Dream Exam draws to a close and the candidates awaken from their slumber, I feel a sense of quiet satisfaction wash over me. For I have borne witness to the birth of a new generation of reapers – twenty-five sinners and twenty-five saints, each one a beacon of hope and judgement.

Yes, the gods rejoiced at their creation, our creation. However, not all shared the same amount of happiness in this celebration. The Goddess of Nature, who had vehemently opposed the creation of the *torva messor*, remained deeply troubled. Ignored and dismissed, her grief grew until she could no longer sustain herself.

In her sorrow, the Goddess of Nature withered away. Though her form was lost, her spirit left a tangible mark upon our realm. This essence is most poignant in the academy's greenhouse; a place where flowers flourish, even when plucked out over and over again.

I've spent many afternoons in this greenhouse, surrounded by blossoms of every hue. Each flower is a testament to the Goddess of Nature's enduring spirit, a reminder of her unheeded warnings and the price of divine hubris. The flowers seem to defy mortality itself, a quiet rebellion against the inevitability of decay. Their resilience inspires me, a symbol of renewal amidst the weighty responsibilities we bear.

Despite the goddess's disappearance, the success of the *torva messor* cannot be denied. We have become skilled shepherds of souls, guiding the departed with both empathy and impartiality. We, sinners and saints, have earned our abilities and found our place within the grand tapestry of existence. Miniscule beings, yes, but part of something essential.

Yet, even in our success, we must remember the lessons of our origins. The Goddess of Nature's plight is a reminder of the consequences of divine oversight. As we carry out our duties, we must strive to honour her legacy, to heed the delicate equilibrium she fought so hard to protect. The flowers in the greenhouse teach us that even in the face of loss, life finds a way to persist and thrive. It is a lesson I carry with me as I walk the fine line between realms.

And so, the story of the reapers continues, each of us a thread of fate. The *Academiae Fatorum* remains our sanctuary, a place of learning, reflection and growth. Here, we forge our path forward, guided by the wisdom of those who came before and the everblooming flowers of the Goddess of Nature.

The following commentary has been written by Master Reaper James in 1982 and added to the 414rd edition of History of the Overworld.

I wish I had the words to express what's it like to be here. I don't have them. To the younger reapers: here's a nugget of wisdom for you. When guiding souls, remember to keep your own soul in check – lest you find yourself in the very predicament of those you're supposed to guide. After all, it's bad enough dealing with the living's baggage.

Keep your wits sharp and your heart even sharper.

The following commentary has been written by Master Reaper Aurelia in 1594 and added to the 263rd edition of History of the Overworld. *May she reincarnate in peace.*

As I sit in the quiet solitude of the Library of Eternities, my thoughts drift to a tale that has long fascinated me – a tale that has been whispered among reapers for centuries, passed down through the ages like a secret. It is the tale of the first sinner and the first saint, and the weapon they wielded: The Scythe.

The Scythe is unlike any other weapon in existence – a divine instrument forged by the hands of the God of Fire and Metal. With a single blow, it can destroy errant spirits and send them into the void beyond. Its power is unmatched, its purpose sacred.

But with great power comes great responsibility, and the Scythe is no exception. Only master reapers can summon it. To wield it is to walk a dangerous path, for as one holds the Scythe for too long, their hand turns as black as coal – a permanent mark, a punishment for abuse of power.

There are records of reapers who have disintegrated entirely from the overuse of the Scythe. Their bodies consumed by the very power they sought to wield. It is a fate I would not wish upon anyone. I bear witness to the truth of this punishment, for I still carry the scar from my last use. The memory of that moment is seared into my mind; the weight of the weapon in my hand, the surge of power coursing through me and the agonising pain as my hand began to wither and decay.

And so, I caution my fellow reapers to tread with forethought when it comes to the Scythe. I beg of you, use it only as last resort, when all other options have been exhausted. Its power is not to be taken without thought, and the consequences of misuse are dire indeed.

We are entrusted with the souls of the departed, with guiding them to their final resting place. And though the temptation of power may be great, we must not lose sight of our true mission, nor the delicate balance we strive to maintain in the realms of life and death.

The following pages contain my notes on a new weapon. *The Chain Sickle.*

33

The following commentary has been written by Master Reaper Grace in 2109 and added to the 486th edition of History of the Overworld.

Ican see why James hated this place so much. May he reincarnate in peace.

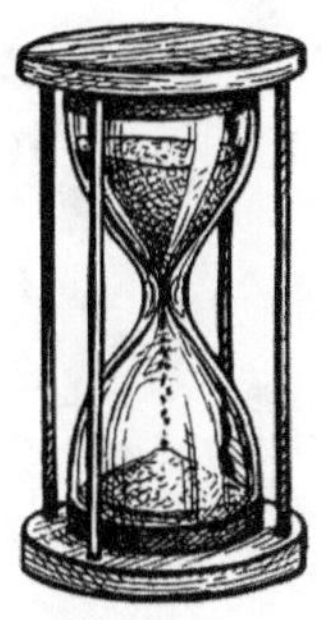

ROADKILL

'Jason Choi, born on the eighteenth of August 1977, aged forty-eight. I've come to collect you.'

The smoke from the hood of the grey liftback was dissipating by the time the police and ambulance arrived. The roadway was uncrowded. Cars rarely passed by in the wee hours of the night. The headlights and the moon were better than any road lighting nearby, which desperately needed a bulb change.

A man's eyes were fixed on the scene as the paramedics extracted a woman his age from the crumpled car. She looked fragile, her face pale against the darkness of the night. His heart skipped a beat, adrenaline coursing through him as he took a hesitant step forward, wanting to reach out, to reassure himself that she was alright.

'Mr. Choi,' again, that honeyed voice.

The man turned around, following the siren-like sound. A silhouette in black came into his view. The stranger stepped forward. The sound of heels was the only thing he could clearly hear. The voices and distant sirens faded in the background as if time suddenly stopped or everything was underwater.

The woman's face was pallid, almost bone-like. She looked around a decade younger than him. Her entire attire – heels, pants, blouse and blazer – had the same tone of charcoal. The only thing that contrasted with her monochrome appearance was her shoulder-length hair. It was wavy, midnight blue, with turquoise streaks. It looked like the ocean. His hands itched to fix his battered denim jacket at her appearance.

'W-who…' Jason gasped. 'How do you know my name?'

'I'm here to escort you,' the mysterious woman replied.

'Escort? What, where?'

'To the Afterlife.'

'What?' he questioned again in complete disbelief. He shook his head in denial. The entire situation had to be a dream.

It felt like a dream. A nightmare. He wanted to believe he was not there. Nothing made sense. But, somehow, his feet were glued to the ground, as if the mere presence of the woman standing before him was pulling him away from reality.

'Look,' she motioned with her head to the front, right at the car.

Jason turned his head to the back to watch the paramedics roll the stretcher. A man was lying down on it. But not just any man. Jason saw himself more tattered and bruised. Dry blood was stuck on his shirt and left ear. He saw himself pale. Deadly pale.

'I-I can't,' Jason stammered. Cold. He felt so cold. 'My wife—'

'She'll live,' the woman interrupted. 'She has a few years of hardship ahead. But she'll be handsomely rewarded. Now, let's go.'

'Go where?'

'Like I said, I'm here to escort you,' she repeated, her tone as calm as a river. One tap of her heel to the ground was the sole indication of her desire to leave. 'I'll take you through the road to the Afterlife.'

The woman motioned to the roadway south. 'This way.'

Jason had no other choice but to follow. He walked, resigned to his fate, two steps behind—

'Who are you?' he blurted out.

'Can't you tell?' The woman's unnatural silver eyes bored into him. 'I'm a reaper.'

Of course, Jason thought. *Escorts. Grim reapers. Jeosung saja. Angels of Death.* They were all the same. So there is something after one dies, then.

'You said my wife would have a hard time in the future. How do you know?'

'We have the ability of knowing how many years a person will live, what kind of life and how many reincarnations they will have.'

'Reincarnations?'

'You will see your wife again,' the reaper assured him. 'I know that's what you truly want to ask. Don't think too much about it. Your lives are tied by fate, so you will meet. No matter when or how.'

'Good,' Jason breathed out. 'That's good.'

For a while, no one uttered a single word. Jason followed the endless road, with fog covering the horizon, three steps behind the reaper, who walked with her arms folded behind her back, a dull purple crystal in her hand. There were no cars on sight. No sound of crickets, either. The road lights were no longer flickering. In fact, they were more luminous than ever. The path was not bumpy like he had noticed when he was driving. It could have been a figment of his imagination. He had crashed the car against a tree for falling asleep. Guilty, as the last memory of his life returned to the front of his mind, Jason felt the urge to turn around. But the reaper had given him one command.

Don't look back.

So instead, he went back to recall his life right before

this moment. Did he do everything he hoped to achieve? His life had been monotonous at first, nothing notorious to point out. He was born to a middle-class family, where they taught him that studies came above all else. They wanted him to thrive in life and have a better outcome than them. With that raising method, he was forced to spend most of his time locked in his bedroom. There was even a particular day when he was not allowed to have dinner until he learned all the irregular verbs by heart. He was not allowed to go out on the weekends unless he had no exams for the upcoming month. And those moments were scarce.

Jason was a slow study, he had to admit. But all that hard work eventually paid off. High school was decorated with straight A's, which granted him entry to prestigious universities: Oxford, Manchester, Birmingham. The list could have been longer if the school system had allowed him to apply to more. He considered schools in the United States, but knew his parents could not afford it. He didn't even attempt to satisfy his curiosity.

But he was overjoyed he stayed. It was how he met the love of his life: Winnie. They shared all of their first-year classes and a couple from year two onwards. They liked comparing notes. Jason was terrible at Administrative Law, but Winnie wasn't. And Jason would tutor her in Family Law.

It was no surprise to the study group when they got married after graduation. Their wedding was perfect, at least according to his eyes, and their honeymoon, even better, as he got to visit Venice for the first time. It had been on his list for quite a long time. Eight years later, three years after moving to a larger apartment in Harrow, they had two beautiful children. They had wanted to wait to become parents. A focus on their careers and their life together was a priority. And he enjoyed watching their sons grow every day. He appreciated every spare second he had with them. Today they had been returning from their eldest son's graduation party. He felt a sense of relief to know that their sons were staying with their grandmother at Watford tonight instead of returning with them.

Had he truly done everything he had hoped to achieve? No. He wanted to see his eldest go to university and his youngest graduate. He wanted to be there for their weddings if they had any. He wanted to grow old with his wife and travel with her around the world. There were so many plans they had still on their travel list, like Niagara Falls or visiting his grandparents in Seoul and going back to the Santorini beaches. But did he enjoy his life as short as it may have been?

Absolutely, yes.

Jason wondered how far they were going to walk, what kind of place they would reach and what punishment he would receive. And, oh, how he hated silence. The intrigue would kill him if he were not dead already. He glanced once more at the crystal and noted it was glowing brighter than before.

'Sorry, um, miss…?' Jason began.

'You can call me Henley,' she replied.

'Okay, miss Henley. What, um…' he trailed off. Henley revealed nothing, her eyes on the road. She did not tell him to carry on with the question.

After a few attempts at opening his mouth to speak and regretting it, he tried again. 'Were you always a reaper? I mean, were you born that way?'

'Reapers were all humans, at least once. Sometimes they become reapers after a great sin.'

That was not comforting. 'And what sin did you commit?'

Henley did not answer. Such time had gone by, Jason concluded she would not say anything else, but then—

'I don't remember.'

'You don't?'

The reaper didn't reply, so Jason tried again.

'Why not?'

'I only have one moment. A dream. Maybe I just imagined it, but it looked so vivid to me. So real. Water, salt, suffocation, despair. I was falling to the darkest parts of the sea,' she recalled. Her face did not denote sadness or sorrow. The reaper did not seem to mind revealing such a story to a stranger.

'Some have the misfortune of remembering their past life. Others don't,' she finished.

'Misfortune,' Jason frowned.

'What if you committed a deadly sin? One you deeply regretted. Wouldn't you want that memory to burn forever? I'm considered one of the lucky ones. But I don't think so. Even in death, people love to judge you.'

'And you don't believe you're lucky?'

The reaper turned her head to him, her lips curving upwards, and Jason wondered if that was the only way she could smile. 'I do hate staying in the dark. My life, no matter the kind, has been ripped away from me. I'd like it back.'

Jason nodded slowly. 'Maybe you will in time.'

'Oh, I plan to.'

Her ankles were wet and throbbing when she returned to the Academy of Fates.

Henley had used the water portal in river Colne. It was an hour's walk from the accident. Her feet hurt like hell, as if she weren't there already. To her relief, other reapers did not seem to notice her as she half limped across the

Grand Atrium. They would rather stare at the pristine marbled columns that adorned the room, or perhaps the star adorned ceiling, instead of her.

She was just one more of the bunch.

Her mentor, James, however, was indeed staring at her as he stood next to the floating holographic map situated in the middle of the room with his arms crossed. The look he was giving her could send shivers down her spine if she were not as exhausted as she was at the moment.

Was he looking at her like that because she had failed the Moon Trial?

'What took you so long?' Her mentor asked.

Henley took a deep breath as she gathered her thoughts. Looking nervous while being assessed would do her no good. She glanced at the number displayed above the intricately detailed map of the United Kingdom, where each region shimmered with its own unique aura, pulsing with the energy of its inhabitants.

67,916,215

The digits danced with life, changing every minute or two. Below the display, a clock ticked away. This was no ordinary timer; it revealed the tally of deaths per day.

994

There were around 1,800 deaths per day, give or take, and that was only the United Kingdom. At the bottom of the mark there were other population clocks of what one would label as 'the great power countries': The United States, Japan, China and the newest addition that everyone here seemed to abhor: The Republic of Ireland. No one here liked to talk about that topic, and Henley knew better than to pry. Best to leave it untouched.

'There is no water in the middle of nowhere.' Henley muttered.

'You could use someone's bathtub.'

She turned to him with a glare. 'Very funny.'

'No, I'm serious,' the mentor went on. 'Any pool of water would do to get you back to the academy. I thought you knew that.'

'Well, I was not going to get into a stranger's home.'

'And who's going to notice?' He raised an eyebrow. 'You could try to knock on the door, but no one would answer. And if they do, because of some rare sixth sense, they're not going to see you unless they are about to die. And that would be a coincidence.'

'Has that happened before?' Henley asked as she took off her heels, no longer caring about formality. Reapers were meant to wear formal clothing at all times. It denoted respect not only to superiors but also to the souls that they were tasked to guide to the Afterlife. Black was also mandatory, as it was the standard symbol of the Overworld. The only colour that she was exempted from removing were her blue locks. It was not something that she wanted to remove; she had grown attached to her style. As for her attire, she wished she could complain about the heels she was forced into. It was not that easy to chase a soul without stumbling. Not that she had the honour and opportunity to do that yet. So far this had been her first encounter with a dead soul. And she thanked the heavens she was lucky enough to finish this trial. Failure was not an option; she would have ceased to exist.

'In those cases, just call. They'll send the proper reaper.'

'You have phones?'

'You earn one once you pass the Moon Trial. So...' The mentor held out his hand. 'Let's see how you did.'

Henley let out a sigh and took out a golden hourglass from her onyx blazer. The sand had already reached the bottom. In the bottom of the hourglass, Jason's name and date of birth were engraved.

The mentor examined the hourglass with a clinical eye. It was as if he could see the dead soul's memories that way. And she believed he could. She had been able to take glimpses of Jason's lifetime. His childhood, his time at school, his wedding and finally his death. But that was because she was holding another element in her hand as he led Jason to the Afterlife. An element that she also handed to her mentor after he finished examining the hourglass. It was a mauve coloured crystal. It was cool and smooth to the touch despite its ridges. It offered a comforting sensation while she held it, as it was filled with Jason's happy memories. She only hoped her mentor wouldn't notice how long it took her to fill those memories into the crystal, or that she wouldn't be marked down if he did.

Good thing Jason was up for walking.

'What do you think Jason Choi's outcome will be?' The mentor turned his head towards her.

Henley stared. Was he testing her? And by the look on his face, she guessed he was. This was her time to answer correctly, or all her training this last three months would go to waste. Would she be shunned out of the academy if she answered wrong?

'Reapers do not have an opinion,' she asserted. 'We are only entities that lead souls to the Afterlife. What happens to them after that is only up to the Fates.'

The girl saw how his lips curved into a slight grin. 'Congratulations, Miss Henley. You have officially passed the first stage of the training. You are free of theoretical lessons.'

'Thank the gods,' Henley mumbled in relief. But the expression of her superior made her correct herself. 'I mean, thank you.'

'You have to work on your stoic face a bit more,' he quipped. 'But look at you, speaking in plural. You are becoming one of us.'

Blending in was something Henley was not fond of. It meant she was becoming one of the black-suit workers. But maybe she was exaggerating. She had learned that the Afterlife did not harbour a god called God. The names, however, were trickier. They were not revealed even when asked. Superiors withheld that kind of information. And that made her wonder if names harboured something more important than just a way to address a person.

It reminded her of a movie that she had seen when she was younger. Or at least, that was what she figured. It was about a little girl who arrived in a spirit world and had her name stolen. With her name, her memories also faded. It had robbed her of her identity. Without her identity, she could be easily manipulated.

Was that also the way things worked here?

When she asked her mentor about it, he had told her that the information was above his clearance.

Bloody hierarchy.

'Does this mean I'm free?' Henley asked.

'You get more free time, yes,' he clarified. 'You are not allowed to interact with mortals nor use your combat magick unless authorised. Oh, and curfew.'

'Right,' Henley nodded.

'And put your shoes back on. You're still bound to the rules of etiquette.'

'You try walking in five-inch heels for hours,' she grumbled, but put them back on, anyway.

'And I'm still your superior.'

At that point, she made the decision to cease her complaints. Sass-talking him in such a public space would not make a good impression.

'I have a question.'

'Fire away.'

'What is the point of passing this trial alone when reapers collect in pairs?'

Her mentor placed his hands on the pocket of his coat and paused. 'A few reasons. First, you need to get acquainted with both elements. And time constraints prevent us from making you collect two souls and allows for make-up test should you fail one of them.'

'Make-up test? Seriously?' Henley raised her eyebrow.

Her mentor waved her off. 'Competition is another motive. Some tend to take this as some sort of way to make an impression and make it look they are better than the rest. Two centuries ago, the Head of the Academy put that to the test, and trainees saw it as means to compete with their partner instead of learning teamwork. After that monumental failure we had to redo the trials and therefore wasted a whole month.'

'And that magically does not happen once you're effective?'

'You'll get to learn more about teamwork during this upcoming trimester and about the downsides of not doing a proper job with a partner. Things can go south if you don't trust one another.'

'Huh… and who's your partner?'

'I don't have one anymore.'

Henley blinked and tilted her head. She thought being partnered was a rule. 'Why not?'

'I'm a mentor now, and I lead a couple of teams. I either assign a pair or do it on my own whenever we are short staffed. And lately that's quite frequent. That's where you and your group come in. If there's any hope to your abilities, you might even tip the scales in our favour.'

'Against errant spirits?'

'Yes, Ma'am. The Overworld is plagued by them. The only cause of our unpredictable demise. Excited for it?'

'Not really.'

Her mentor grinned. 'Good.'

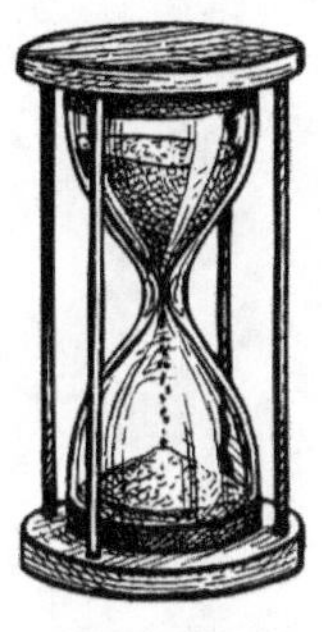

SENSES

Blurry, cloudy, dark. *The smell of incense filled her nostrils. The sound of steps against the wooden ground reached her ears. The taste of musky, sweet liquor passed her lips and tongue. The feel of a sharp blade slashed through her fingertips. The sight of the largest moon she had ever seen embedded her brain. A flash of images – a queue of people walking through a wet, sandy path, her rough feet reaching a ship made of cedar and red oak, footsteps echoing behind her, blood oozing out from—*

A small gasp escaped her lips. With a shiver rippling down her spine, she found herself abruptly awake, the remnants of her unsettling vision still haunting her senses. Her hands, buried beneath the embrace of the linen sheets, felt cold and numb against her skin. The young woman blinked, adjusting her eyes to her dark bedroom. She remained rooted to her spot, unable to muster the strength to stretch or move from her side position. Every muscle in her body felt as if it were encased in lead, weighed down by the lingering tendrils of sleep that clung to her limbs. Her mind swirled with the remnants of her unsettling dream. She could not shake the feeling of unease that lingered like a shadow in the recesses of her consciousness.

The taste of musky, sweet liquor still lingered on her tongue. And the memory of the sharp sting of the blade against her fingertips sent a shiver coursing through her body. The sensations were all too real.

With trembling fingers, she reached for her cell phone, the glow of the screen casting an eerie light across her darkened bedroom.

3:33

The numbers stared back at her; a reminder of the sleepless nights that had become all too familiar. For the past months vivid images had plagued her mind during times of rest. The girl somehow knew those visions were not figments of her imagination, but visions. Memories. And the question that kept her awake until sunrise.

Who was the one dying in her arms?

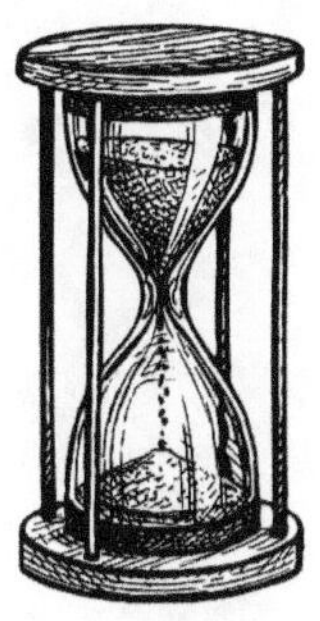

GATHERING

'So, tell us, how did things become so jumbled?'

The old lady's voice disrupted the harmony of the tea. This was a sight that not many got the honour to witness – the gatherings of the Fates. Once every new moon they would cease from their unstoppable tasks and have tea at their little garden. Nestled within reality's folds, their garden was a tranquil oasis where destiny's blooms flourished. Flowers, with petals as white as starlight, unfurled their delicate blossoms. Enchanted vines climbed lattice walls adorned with tiny silver bells that chimed softly with every passing breeze.

In the centre stood a structure of intertwining branches and shimmering threads where Past, Present and Future worked in harmony. Stone pathways meandered through lush greenery, leading to secluded alcoves where ancient tomes containing the secrets of time and destiny rested.

This garden would envelop the Fates in a cocoon of serenity, shielding them from the chaos of the world beyond. As for these encounters, they would have to stop time, as the lives of the humans could not be left unattended. It was true humans had free will. Yet, the Fates existed to oversee humanity's destinies.

And at those particular nights, the sisters would discuss their progress. Tonight, however, they would discuss failures.

Humanity's failures.

'Such an antique word, darling. And not so specific. You can say "fucked up",' Past cackled. 'Don't worry about *me*.'

'Oh, don't be so crass,' Present wrinkled her nose in annoyance. 'These kids say "fuck up" for anything nowadays. There is no need to be like them.'

'It's called being modern, isn't that right?'

'It's called following the boring flock.'

'Silence!' Future's voice boomed loud and clear. 'I did not summon you to watch you throttle each other all day. It is exhausting, and I have no time for it.'

Past and Present looked at each other before looking to their youngest sister.

'Apologies, Future Sister.'

'Yes, yes, apologies.'

'I swear, being stuck with you in eternity is not heavenly,' Future scoffed. She leaned to take a cup of tea from the small round table and took a sip, taking her time to savour its fruity taste.

'Anyway,' she carried on. 'We are gathered here today to discuss the recent events that occurred in the United Kingdom over the last century. We had to witness countless conflicts, either political or territorial, that I will not even mention today. Two world wars which, even though expected, were exhausting and caused numerous complaints from the Overworld.

'They said they were short staffed,' Past supplied.

'That's what they said, yes.'

'The Head of the Academy could not take it anymore,' Present shook her head. 'So, she sent for representatives from the neutral countries to help with the task. A sensitive approach if you ask me.'

'So many conflicts of jurisdiction as well.'

'There are protocols for that,' Future reminded Past.

'To be honest, I felt sorry for the lands that were actually invaded in those wars,' Present lamented.

'Is that meant to be a joke? They lost Ireland!'

'Right, yes, sorry.'

'Many reapers did not know what the hell to do during those times. Fights for territory down there meant conflicts for us.'

'Them, Past Sister. Them,' Future corrected Present. 'We merely watch.'

That made the middle sister cackle. 'Watching the Irish Head cat fight with the English one? Yes, that was entertaining.'

'No, it wasn't. Newly appointed headmasters are an absolute pain. In fact, we should say something about these random selections. They don't know what they are doing. The Irish Head did not even know who truly belonged in his territory.'

'Don't change the subject, Future Sister. You have to admit the whole situation made you smile, even a tiny bit.'

'Must have been your imagination, Present Sister.'

'I still remember it as clear as day.'

Future let out a frustrated sigh. If she kept arguing with Present, the night would be wasted and so would this gathering. 'Could we just focus for a moment? Discussing how we felt during those conflicts is not the main issue here.'

Past shrugged. She had no care for the lives that were lost. 'Well, what is there to discuss? People die all the time. Invasions, wars, independence, diseases—'

'Yes,' Present let out a sigh. 'Let us not forget about the pandemic.'

'The *influenza*, yes. Another disastrous event. The point is people die. The cause matters not. And we select who is meant to walk into the Afterlife depending on the actions of each person.'

'I did not come here to discuss whether we should cut more or less threads.' Future pinched the bridge of her nose. At least they could agree to the fact that the birth-death ratio was more than adequate. Overpopulation in some countries was expected in a couple of decades. 'We will if we deem it fit. The problem lies somewhere else.'

Silence sliced through the air. Present and Past looked at each other for a brief moment.

'You don't mean…' Present trailed off.

'Yes.'

'Gods, no, why?' Past stomped her foot on the stoned ground.

'That problem you are thinking about solely lies on the reapers' responsibility.'

'Oh, yes,' Future rolled her eyes at her sister's antics. One would say they behaved like children. 'Blame it on the reapers. They have too many unwilling souls dying in the first place. Too many becoming errant spirits – they don't choose who or how many humans die! We do. It's our fault.'

'It is not our fault!' Present crossed her arms. 'The souls chose to do this, and that is out of our control.'

'And yet, it is our responsibility to take these matters into our own hands.'

'Well, we shall do no such thing. That is not our role in the world. We only decide each human's lifetime. That is all. Whatever they do after they meet death remains solely the responsibility of the *torva messor*.'

'Errant spirits cannot run about in the Overworld, Past Sister. Their souls are contaminated with dark magick, the only tool that can kill reapers. And without reapers—'

'Every single soul becomes an errant spirit,' Present interrupted. 'And that means—'

'No reincarnation and no more births,' Past finished. 'How exhausting.'

'So, yes. It is our responsibility,' Future gave them a look that screamed *I told you so*.

'So, what do you suggest?'

'That's a great question. I summoned you here for this very reason.'

'Oh, for the gods' sake,' Past let out, her patience wearing thin. 'You don't have an idea yet? Have we just wasted this afternoon completely?'

'I do not think so, truth be told. This red elderberry tea is just wonderful,' Present remarked, finding solace in simple pleasures.

'Silence!' Future's voice echoed through the Destiny Room. She was the most volatile of the trio and did not tolerate their banters, which were too frequent for her liking. 'You're giving me a headache!'

Past and Present, finding amusement in their younger sister's outburst, exchanged a knowing glance. 'Apologies, sister,' they offered half-heartedly. They could tease their youngest for all eternity and never grow tired of it.

Future let out an exasperated sigh, tired of dealing with them so soon after the first round of tea being served. And yet, she had been bound to remain with them since the moment they had been created. Humans referred to them by many names. Many believed that they were distinct entities, and others thought they did not exist at all. But they were one and the same. The *Moirai*. The *Parcae*. The Fates – ancient and eternal beings born from the very fabric of existence itself. In the primordial chaos of the universe's birth, they emerged as three distinct entities, each embodying a fundamental aspect of destiny.

Past, the spinner of life's threads, came into being first. With delicate fingers, she wove the strands of mortal lives into the grand tapestry of fate. At her side stood Present, the measurer of destiny, who determined the length and course of each thread with precision. Together, they resided in the timeless realm of the Destiny Room, where the infinite threads of existence converged.

At the heart of this celestial domain sat Future, the cutter of life's threads. It was she who wielded the shears of finality, severing the threads when the appointed time came to an end.

Past, Present, and Future, the manifestations of time itself, served as witnesses to the unfolding of events across the ages. They were bound together in an eternal dance, their roles intertwined yet distinct. While Past reminisced in memories long gone, Present savoured each fleeting moment, and Future gazed ahead with eyes that pierced the veils of possibility.

Despite their differences, the Fates were irrevocably linked, intertwined like the threads they manipulated. And so, even as each of them abhorred each other's complaints, they knew they were forever bound to one another.

The *torva messor*, however, were an entirely different matter. And as Future was one of the main involved in their creation, she could not help but feel attached to those miserable and overworked creatures. After a pause only meant for slurping tea and munching biscuits, she spoke up. 'We have a Blood Moon this month, isn't that right?'

'It happens every hundred years, sissy. I don't know why you're still asking the same thing every century.'

'I have a point to make this time.'

'Oh, do you, now?'

'Yes, yes, I'm getting there. We have the Blood Moon every century—'

'I have never understood why we don't hire new reapers whenever the new century begins,' Past interrupted, looking at the embroidered napkins.

'Because Blood Moons can only be summoned in the winter's solstice,' Future replied.

'That's not what I meant.'

'I know that. Blood Moons can only be summoned in the winter's solstice, *and* reapers begin their training with the birth of the new century. Since we are in the northern hemisphere, we are bound to do it on the December of the previous year unlike the ones in the southern hemisphere, where they do it six months after.'

Present tapped her fingers. 'Are we getting to a point?'

Future pointed her long nails at her middle sister. 'Well, if you let me bloody speak! We get fifty new reapers every hundred years, twenty-five sinners and twenty-five saints. Now the number diminishes every year. Either they die because of errant spirits, or they choose to reincarnate as they do not want to meet the same fate.'

'Cowards. The lot of them,' Past grumbled.

'No, you would do the same.'

'So, let's summon the blood moon more frequently,' Future said.

'Excuse me?'

'There is a balance to everything, little sissy. You cannot expect us to just summon the blood moon whenever we feel like it.'

'Or, more like, whenever our little sister feels like it. After all, it's her idea.'

'No, but we still have the power to change the law temporarily, perhaps for this century only, and see if the numbers between reapers and errant spirits become more balanced.'

'What do you propose?'

Future scratched her chin, pondering. She focused her gaze on the nearby blooming flowers. Negotiation with her sisters would be hard. She should come up with a reasonable number. 'Five years.'

'Well, that's just preposterous,' Present shook her head. 'The Head will not stand for it. And the mentors will have their hands full. I say fifty.'

'Ten.'

'Forty-five!'

'How about thirty?'

'Forty!'

'Twenty-five,' Future uttered in a tone that had no room to counteroffers. 'We will do twenty-five. Starting from the next quarter of the century. That will be during the Winter Solstice that marks the beginning of 2025. Objections?'

Past cleared her throat, looking away. She shook her head. 'No, I guess not.'

'No,' Present mumbled before taking a sip of tea.

Future folded her hands together in front of the table. Her hard expression turned into a pleased one. 'Good. I will write a letter to the Head of the Academy myself so she can begin the arrangements.'

'She won't like this sudden change.'

'But we don't really care what she likes, do we?'

'She can be easily replaced if she so much as whines about it. Remember, to reapers, we are the messengers of the gods.'

'Can you imagine?' Past giggled. 'The academy they will be running around already. Ensuring the cabins are ready to receive the sleeping souls into their realm, preparing the tools for the Dream Exam, adjusting the schedule for training—'

'Well, that's nothing, big sister,' Present gushed. 'They need to hurry and gather all the souls that are meant to be dying that year. How much would that be? Around eleven thousand?'

'14,714 souls between the ages of eighteen and thirty will die in the region that year, to be exact,' Future confirmed.

'A very fine number.'

Past nodded in approval. 'Yes, yes, I agree.'

'And to be fair, we are giving them time. After all, some of those selected souls are already born. The reapers can begin the gathering of their crystals and hourglasses.'

'I suppose so,' Present conceded, but her tone was not as confident as she thought it would come out. She doubted the efficacy of this new experiment. Should it go wrong, there would be no point in the souls lost. Should it go right, they would have to apply it to the rest of the world. Busier years were ahead of them, as if they did not have too much on their plate already.

The Fates agreed that humans could be exhausting. Sometimes overwhelmingly so with their desire to live longer and have more than what they deserved. Over the centuries, they had witnessed the insatiable hunger of mortals, their endless pursuit of power and wealth often leading to despair. Yet, despite their flaws, the Fates made compassionate decisions for humanity. They sought to understand the fragility of mortal life. And so, when the need arose, they intervened with a gentler hand.

One such intervention was an extended life expectancy, which kept a steady rise over the last century. As mortal civilisations evolved and progressed, the Fates recognised the need for longevity to fulfil their potential. They adjusted the threads of fate, nudging the course of events to allow for longer, healthier lives. It was not a decision taken without thought, for every alteration to the fabric of destiny carried consequences. By granting humanity more time, they could foster greater wisdom, compassion and understanding. They had been generous enough to extend the expectancy from seventy to almost eighty. Yet they still wanted more?

How ungrateful.

Such gifts came with challenges. Extended lifespans meant new tribulations, as mortals grappled with the weight of time and the burden of memory. And that was how the number of souls in the Netherworld increased by tenfold.

'Then why are you making a face?' Future asked.

'Forgive me for being slightly concerned about the fact that things might not go as flawlessly as you are predicting, sister.'

'Future is unpredictable,' she shrugged, as if she had just admitted it was in her nature. And perhaps it was. 'That's what got us into this mess. Consider this an experiment. Should it go wrong, then we shall discuss it again. But there's one thing I'm sure about.'

The Fates of the Past and Present turned to her youngest. 'And what is that?'

Future could not help but grin. 'A sprinkle of chaos might just be exactly what this world needs.'

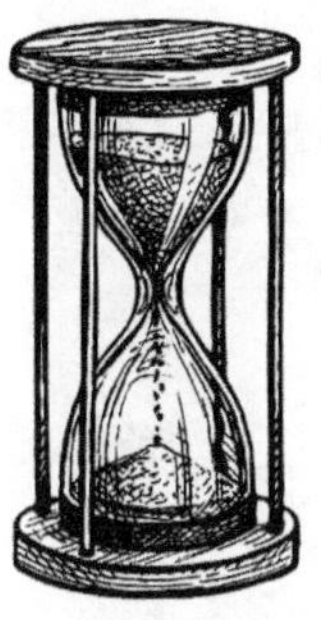

FALLING

It is said that reapers have existed since the origin of mankind. But no reaper has worked that long to tell the tale. They have chased souls across lands and seas, intently watching their final moments until their last breath.

Such a rare case, this one. This one who would later be a server of the Fates. He was a dreamer, an adventurer. A pirate they called Dyer.

At first, he had taken tentative steps. He didn't know the way of the world. Of trade. Of gamble. Of self-conniving trash. Now, with one-and-twenty years of age, he strolled with confidence through the crowded black market, used to the smells and the noises of the blacksmiths forging weapons. The gunner manoeuvred through the bustling throngs of people with a leather pouch of coins clutched in his hand. He approached one of the stalls, its wooden counter laden with an array of goods. The merchant behind the stand and the gunner exchanged pleasantries as they counted out the coins.

'Thanks,' Dyer muttered, his voice almost inaudible over the din of the crowd, as he received a small parcel in return.

A tap on his shoulder drew his attention, and he turned to look at another fellow trader with a knowing smirk on his face. *Lewis.* They exchanged a nod of recognition before the gunner's curiosity led him to a neighbouring stall adorned with an eclectic assortment of gloves and other accessories.

'How much for the watches?' Dyer inquired, his gaze lingering on the jewellery displayed before him.

'Thirty pieces per watch,' Lewis replied.

Dyer's eyebrows shot up. 'What? Some of those were made of gold,' he protested.

Lewis shrugged, his expression conveying a nonchalant acceptance of the market's unpredictable pricing. 'Some shit about a conflict with the British Crown and inflation.'

'Ridiculous,' Dyer murmured under his breath.

A gleaming silver necklace adorned with a vibrant, teardrop-shaped sapphire soon captured his attention, nestled amidst a sea of trinkets and baubles. Its elegant design caught the sunlight, casting a mesmerising glow that beckoned to him.

'Would you like to take it up to the vendor?'

'No, thank you.' His fingers itched to reach out and claim the exquisite piece.

Lewis observed his friend's growing fascination with the necklace. 'Mate? No,' he warned. Ever the voice of reason and killjoy.

Yet Dyer remained undeterred, his spirit undiminished as he envisioned the necklace adorning the neck of a special someone. 'I think she'll look great in it, don't you think?'

Lewis shook his head. 'You want to swim with the sharks tonight? 'Cause that's what's going to happen to you.'

But Dyer only chuckled, brushing off Lewis's concerns with a wave of his hand. 'Relax. She won't know it's from me.'

'Sure. It's not like the entire crew knows,' he quipped.

Dyer paused. 'Am I that obvious?'

'Yes. Also? You can't afford it,' he ventured.

'Yes, I can.'

'No, you can't. Put it back.' Lewis made a futile attempt to snatch the necklace from his grasp.

'Stop that.' Dyer extended his arm, shoving Lewis away as he turned back to the merchant with a grin. 'Wrap it for me?'

The Duchess sliced through Atlantic, her majestic form gleaming in the sunlight as she forged ahead into the boundless expanse of the deep blue sea.

At the heart of the ship, high on the foremast's yardarm, Dyer and Lewis clung to the rigging, gently rocked by the salty breeze. They lashed the topsail, their hands manipulating the ropes as they worked in unison to ensure the sails were secure.

'Oi!' A sharp call from the main deck below shattered the tranquillity of their task. They cast their gaze downward to Tim, one of their shipmates.

'The captain wants to see you.'

Dyer glanced at his friend, a silent exchange passing between them. He turns to Tim, pointing at himself for confirmation.

'Yeah, you, Dyer.'

Suppressing a chuckle, Lewis offered a knowing glance, his amusement evident as he revelled in his earlier prediction.

Closing the door behind him, Dyer stood in the dimly lit cabin, the weight of Captain Morgan's gaze bearing down on him like an anchor. His jaw clenched as he approached her desk, his hands folding behind his back in a gesture of deference. And devotion. Lots of it.

'Captain?' His voice was steady, betraying none of the turmoil swirling within him. His heart clenched at the sight of her, and he wished she wouldn't notice how wild it was beating.

For her. *Only* for her.

'Dyer,' Morgan acknowledged, her tone clipped as she gestured to the necklace lying on the desk. 'What's that?'

Dyer swallowed hard, the lump in his throat threatening to choke him. 'A… necklace?'

'No need to play stupid,' she retorted.

'I'm not…' he began, but her piercing gaze cut through his facade. He cleared his throat. 'It's a token of appreciation for… letting me join your crew.' The words tasted bitter on his tongue. Where did all his courage go?

'That was a year ago,' she waved her hand. Her indifference was a bitter pill to swallow. 'There is no need for this – whatever this nonsense is. It's unpleasant. No more. Understood?'

Dyer nodded, his shoulders sagging. But something within him rebelled at the thought of conceding with such ease.

'I just thought the sapphire would complement your eyes,' he blurted out.

'You forget your place,' she admonished, her tone icy. 'You're a gunner.'

'Do titles matter in circumstances like this?'

'Absolutely.'

'You don't have many fine choices, then.' Dyer grumbled under his breath.

He shouldn't have said that. He noticed how her face contorted. Her narrowed eyes could have pierced a soul, but Dyer was undeterred by her expression.

'I tire of your impertinence, kid,' she snapped, getting a hold of one of the letters on her desk, as if suddenly that was more important than his minuscule presence. 'You'll get kitchen duty until we reach New Providence.'

He swallowed his pride and bowed his head. 'Yes, Captain,' Dyer conceded, the bitterness of failure coating his words. *Why couldn't he just say the words?*

'Good. Dismissed,' she commanded, her tone final.

Turning to leave, Dyer felt her gaze burning into his back. He felt stupid. But before he could make his exit, her voice stopped him in his tracks.

'Wait, take that with you.'

Dyer hesitated for a moment. But he was not trying to decide if he should grab it. There was no way he would take that thing with him. It belonged to her. He was just figuring out what to say.

Unable to resist one final act of defiance, he turned to face her, resolve flashing in his eyes. 'Feel free to dispose of it if you wish. And, Captain? I refuse to give up. Just thought you should know.'

As he left the cabin, her stunned silence lingered behind him.

Later that day, Dyer was submerged in a sea of dirty dishes. He wiped his sweat out of his forehead and dark hair as he scrubbed away the stubborn grime.

Leaning against the door frame, Lewis observed his labour with a mixture of amusement and concern. 'Why do you do this to yourself?'

'Fuck off,' Dyer muttered, his gaze fixed on the task at hand.

But Lewis persisted. He had a way of digging the knife deeper. 'No, mate. I'm serious. You could get any woman you fancy...'

Tightness spread through his chest at his friend's words, his hands freezing mid-scrub as he turned to face

Lewis. No, the day he would get her off his mind would probably be never; he knew for certain that in his next life and the next his heart would recognise her anywhere. 'I don't want another woman.'

The memory of their first encounter was as vivid as if it had happened only yesterday. Dyer had been a nobleman back then, accustomed to luxuries and other privileges befitting his station. But all that changed the night this woman stormed into his life like a tempest, disrupting the very foundation of his existence.

His family had been away, leaving Dyer alone in their grand mansion. He had been reading by the fireplace, the flickering flames casting a warm glow across the room, when the door burst open. A group of rugged individuals flooded in, their eyes scanning the room with a predatory gaze. Among them was her. The captain stood out like a beacon. A fierce, commanding presence that drew everyone's attention and held it captive. Dyer stood entranced as she directed her crew to take what they wanted. Dyer and his staff were brought to their knees, her crew securing the coins and jewels they sought. Her eyes, sharp and calculating, swept over the room. She approached him, her sword pointed at his chin to make him look at her.

Their eyes locked, and Dyer felt as if the world had stopped. There was something in her eyes; something untamed, but also sorrowful. It was in that instant he knew he was lost. Morgan spared his life that night, a gesture that left him at a loss. She took everything of value, including a piece of his heart that he would never reclaim.

Driven by a newfound purpose, Dyer made a choice that defied all reason and societal expectation. He joined her crew. Leaving behind his life of comfort, he embraced the dangers of a pirate's life, all for the chance to be near her. From that day forward, he could not stop thinking about her – her strength, her spirit, her beauty. Every glance, every word exchanged only deepened his infatuation.

'How many times does she have to reject you?'

'She didn't.'

'That's because that shit was expensive. She'll probably sell it,' Lewis scoffed. 'Plus, she is older than you.'

'By only two years!'

'She still thinks you are a child.'

Dyer halted his task, turning to face Lewis with a glare. 'Knock it off.'

'You need to let go,' he urged.

Dyer groaned. He understood Lewis meant well, but he didn't have to be so discouraging. Not when they had gotten to know one another for so long that they could identify each other's snores. They were as thick as thieves after Dyer had offered Lewis sparring lessons every morning, an hour before dawn, because he had noticed his stance was weak. It was Dyer's training that had saved Lewis from many encounters with death.

And death was always on the watch.

'Let me be,' he implored. 'I don't want to give up and keep my head down. I want to risk it. We are sentenced for brief lives here. And when I die, I want to look back and have no regrets.'

The weight of his words hung heavy in the air for a moment. Lewis relented with a silent nod. He might have figured out that it was useless to reason with him.

Lewis threw his hands up in the air. 'Fine.'

With a satisfied nod, Dyer returned his focus to the dishes. Silence ensued between them until Lewis spoiled it again.

'But if she cuts your fingers like she did to that lady that one time,' he added, his tone tinged with humour, 'I won't bandage your hands.'

A small smile tugged at the corners of Dyer's lips. 'I don't wear rings.'

Atlantic Sea, 1716

Should his parents see him now, they would be disappointed. And perhaps that was not the most appropriate word. They would disown him if they had not already. This was not the life that they had planned out for him. But Dyer did not regret a thing. All that hard work had paid off. As time went by, he moved up in ranks.

Despite his successes, there was one area where Dyer's efforts fell short – winning Morgan's heart. No matter how hard he tried to break through her walls, she remained elusive, a ghost haunting the corridors of his mind. Their interactions were few and far between. When Morgan ordered meetings and assigned duties, Dyer had dared to hope that it would bring them closer together, that it would be the opportunity he had been waiting for to prove himself worthy of her affection. But instead, it only pushed her away even more, like a ship drifting ever further from shore, lost in the vast expanse of the sea.

Despite her icy demeanour, Dyer refused to give up hope. He poured himself into his duties, working to the bone to prove he was not only a capable first mate, but a man worthy of Morgan's love. He studied her every move, memorised the sparkle in her eyes, the way her dark waves caught the sunlight as she stood at the quarterdeck. He had vowed to continue his quest to win the captain's affections, no matter the cost.

One day, Dyer was setting course with Lewis at the helm and caught sight of Morgan as she made her way towards her cabin. The sunlight caught the delicate chain around her neck, causing *the* pendant to shimmer in the light. He was sure this was it.

'Dyer, no,' Lewis muttered low, aware of his expression. Too late.

Heart pounding in his chest, Dyer abandoned his task and followed her. Lewis could lead them southeast on his own. He could not help himself as he grabbed her arm and turned her towards him.

Morgan narrowed her eyes. 'What do you want?'

And there it was, the token of his affection wrapped around her neck. Dyer swallowed hard, a knot forming in his throat as he struggled to find the right words. 'You wear blue so well,' Dyer breathed out.

Morgan smacked his hand away. 'Get off me.'

'I was hoping to get on you instead.'

'I'll ignore your crassness this time. And I'll shed a bit of truth, since you're too blind to see it. You really don't want to be with me.'

The sting of rejection burned like a hot coal in his chest. He had hoped that seeing her wearing the necklace would be a sign that she felt the same way he did, that there was a chance for them to be together. But now, as he stood before her, he realised he had been fooling himself all along. Morgan was not his to claim, no matter how much he wished it to be true. That did not mean he was not going to keep trying.

'Why not?'

'Listen, you're not the first. Everyone wants to have a go at one of the very few women of the crew—'

'Are you serious right now?' Dyer scowled. Out of all things, he had not expected to hear that. Damn it, he felt the temperature of his body flare up. *Who dared…?*

'I'm not exactly the woman you should go for,' Morgan continued, uncaring. 'I'm a hassle. You know my father is still on our tail since I turned my back on him. So, death is always watching me.'

'That's bullshit.'

'How's that?'

'Well, first off, you avoid conflict.'

'Excuse me?'

'I'll reword that,' Dyer pointed his index finger at her, wanting to wipe off her glare. 'You don't engage in battles to avoid casualties. You are one of the very few captains that have taken great care of their crew for the past *nine* years. And I think that's admirable. Hell, that's one of the things I really like about you, in fact. Gathering this group at only five-and-ten years old? That—'

'Your point is?'

'Point is, you are the woman I chose. And unless you have another reason—'

'See, I don't need to give you another reason.'

'But I want one!' Dyer's voice tone was now louder than desired. He didn't care if heads were turned his way. Morgan must have noticed; her eyes were wider than usual. 'Considering you're wearing my necklace, and I'm your second—'

'Starting to regret that,' she muttered and looked away.

'Why are you so afraid of saying yes? You want me.'

Morgan scoffed. 'Says who?'

Perhaps this was a bold move towards a captain. But he wanted her to look at him. He got a hold of her jaw and turned her towards him. 'Your eyes. Those beautiful hazel eyes that I fell in love with ever since the moment I saw you. I've seen how you look at me—'

'You're in my line of vision, that's all.' She glared at him.

And yet, she did not pull away from him.

'You took care of me when I was wounded.'

'Oh, please, it's not like I've never healed a crewmate before.'

'In your quarters?' She had nursed him back to health. Even in his feverish state, he still recalled how she had changed the bandages and placed cold compresses into his skin. God, he would take a bullet for this woman. 'So? What else are you going to deny, Morgan?'

'*Morgan?*'

'Captain,' Dyer corrected. 'It's just… it feels wrong to call you that way,' he added with a mumble. He was confessing, after all. Again.

'We're not close, Dyer.'

'Let me in, then,' he pleaded. 'I would never hurt you.'

'Anyone can say that.'

'I would never hurt you,' Dyer insisted.

'No, but I would,' Morgan stated.

'No, you wouldn't.'

'Are you sure about that?'

And that was when he felt it. A sharp object poking at his abdomen. He looked down to find her knife. But Dyer could not help but to chuckle. This was all amusing to him. He took another bold step towards her, the knife still pressed on his skin. 'Yes, please, go ahead. Happy to die by your hand.'

'You're crazy.'

'For you? Yes, Ma'am, I am.'

'When are you going to quit this act?'

'Never. What's the point of living if I don't get to be with my other half?'

'Bold of you to assume you know me,' Morgan hissed.

'Oh, I know everything.' Dyer's eyes were hooded as he recalled. 'You want to have a better life on your own, not make others build it for you. That's why you don't get along with your father. I respect that. You hired outcasts in your crew and shaped them into a better version of themselves. Killing is not on your agenda, and you only rob what has already been stolen.'

'Alright, that's enough. I—'

'And if you want to get into specifics?' Dyer went on. 'You like watching sunsets by the window in your cabin. You have an obscene number of rings in your drawer, and your fingers are too small to put them all, but you keep them anyway. You changed the red apples to green ones in the galley because you know I prefer them. You drink a cup of rum at night. And not just any rum they serve at a pub. You like the really aged ones with hints of nuts and vanilla that we can only get in the Caribbean isles.

'You are fierce, loyal, compassionate, even though you would never admit it. And beautiful. So damn beautiful,' Dyer finished with a sigh. 'Can I be yours?'

He could swear there was hesitation in her expression. But was that perhaps his imagination caused by his despair?

'You're playing a dangerous game, Dyer,' she warned, her voice low.

Dyer's eyes did not waver from hers. 'Maybe so, but it's a game worth playing if it means being with you.'

She shook her head, her expression hardening. 'You're delusional. I don't need anyone like you in my life.'

Dyer's face fell, but he didn't back down. 'Maybe not,' he echoed. 'But I'm not giving up on you.'

Morgan's lips tightened into a thin line, and without another word, she turned on her heel and walked away, leaving Dyer with his heart heavy.

His heartbreak did not last for long. He had already waited two years. What was another two? But the Fates surprised him with this turn of events. It was a full moon. The air was cool, tinged with the scent of salt.

Dyer approached Morgan's quarters; a logbook tucked under his arm. It was part of his duties as first mate to deliver the daily records, ensuring that everything was in order for the captain's review. He stopped in his tracks after opening the door.

Inside, Morgan sat at her desk, a half-empty glass of rum in her hand. The flickering candlelight cast shadows across her face; her eyes were weary. She looked up as Dyer entered, her expression guarded but not unkind.

'I apologise. I thought you were still at the helm,' he tried to explain.

'Dyer,' she acknowledged. Her voice did not have the slurred quality he expected. 'What brings you here at this hour?'

'I brought the logbook and the map for our next journey, Captain. I thought you'd want to review them before morning,' Dyer reported, his voice steady. Or at least, that was what he was trying to sound like. He approached her desk, placing the items down with a respectful nod.

Morgan nodded, her fingers tracing the rim of her glass. 'Thank you, Dyer,' she replied, her voice softer than usual. She glanced at the map for a fleet moment before her eyes returned to the amber liquid in her glass.

Dyer took a step back, ready to leave, but his legs were rooted to the place, not wanting to leave so soon.

'Would you like some?' Morgan offered, lifting the bottle of rum.

His heart skipped a beat at the unexpected invitation. 'Sure.'

Morgan stood up to fetch a glass from her cabinet by her desk and poured him the drink, the sound of the liquid filling the silence between them. He took a few steps and took the glass from her.

They stood there for a moment. The tension in the room was palpable, yet somehow comforting. Dyer took a sip, savouring the rich flavours while keeping his eyes on Morgan over the rim of his glass. She looked different tonight, more relaxed.

'I've seen you work hard,' Morgan blurted out of nowhere, her eyes meeting his. 'You've proven yourself time and again. I… appreciate it.'

Dyer's breath caught in his throat. He had longed for any sign of acknowledgement from her, and now, here it was, wrapped in the quiet intimacy of the evening.

'Thank you, Ma'am,' he murmured. 'I would do anything for this ship… and for you.'

Morgan set her glass down on the desk and leaned forward, her eyes searching his. The world outside the cabin ceased to exist, leaving only the two of them in the warm, lantern-lit room. Dyer felt his heart race as Morgan leaned in, her lips brushing against his with surprising tenderness. For a heartbeat, Dyer was lost in the sensation, his long-held desires rushing to the surface. The warmth of her breath, the softness of her lips; it was everything he had dreamed of and more. The moment he had longed for was finally within reach, yet something held him back. As their lips were about to meet again,

Dyer placed a hand on her cheek to stop her, his thumb brushing against her lips.

'Not like this.'

Her brows furrowed in confusion, and her back straightened, pulling back from him. 'What?'

Dyer took a deep breath, gathering his thoughts before speaking. 'You're drunk.'

'I'm not.'

'I can smell the rum.'

'I'm not that drunk. I know what I'm doing.' Her eyes flashed at him.

But Dyer shook his head. 'It doesn't matter. I want this to be right, Morgan. I waited for so long. I can wait until morning.'

She stared at him, her expression a mix of disappointment and something else – something he could not decipher. 'You're serious.'

'I am.'

Morgan turned away from him, her shoulders slumping. For a moment, there was silence, the only sound the gentle lapping of the waves against the hull of the ship. His heart was beating too loud for his liking, as he waited for what she was going to say next. She took hold of her glass and dumped the remaining contents out of her ajar window. 'I'll see you in the morning, Dyer.'

With that, Dyer made his way back to his quarters.

He could not shake the feeling that perhaps he missed the opportunity. Unable to find solace in sleep, he found himself drawn to the helm, seeking refuge in the quiet solitude of the early morning hours. With arms braced against the railing, he gazed out at the horizon, where the first hints of dawn painted the sky in shades of gold and pink. Just as he was lost in contemplation, Morgan's voice shattered the silence, pulling him from his reverie.

'Are you going to reject me again?' Her voice struck a chord deep within him. Turning towards her, the sight of her approaching figure again captivated him. His right hand gripped the rail, as Morgan closed the distance between them.

'I didn't reject you. You, on the other hand—'

But Dyer could not finish the sentence. Her lips were on his, and Dyer's world spun on its axis. It was as if every nerve ending in his body had come alive, every sense heightened to an almost unbearable degree. The touch of her lips against his was electrifying, sending a surge of warmth coursing through his veins.

Her lips were yielding beneath his own, a perfect fit that left him craving more with every passing second. But even as he savoured the taste of her, a part of Dyer couldn't help but wonder if this was real, if it was truly happening or if it was part of his imagination. He felt her fingers cup his jaw, her heartbeat echoing the rhythm of his own. He knew with a certainty that he hadn't felt before this was no dream. It was the beginning of something beautiful and real.

But, as quickly as it had begun, the moment was shattered as she pulled away, leaving Dyer wanting for more. Just as he leaned in, searching for her lips, her voice stopped her.

'If you break it, I'll kill you.' she warned, her eyes searching for his.

Dyer's heart skipped a beat, sobering up at her words. 'Break, what?'

'My heart.'

'Never,' Dyer breathed, his voice a fervent promise as he kissed her again. This time, the kiss was filled with a raw intensity, a desperate longing that had been building between them for far too long. He felt her respond with eagerness, her lips moving against his with a hunger that mirrored his own.

Dyer lifted Morgan up onto the rail, wrapping her legs around his waist. Their kisses grew deeper, more urgent. Dyer's heart pounded in his chest, a symphony of desire and longing that drowned out the sound of the waves.

In that moment, there was only Morgan.

The softness of her lips, the warmth of her touch, the way her body moulded against his as if they were made for each other. His heart was whole again.

Dyer knew with absolute certainty that he would do anything to protect her, no matter how chaotic their lives would be at sea. They could weather any storm that came their way.

Atlantic Sea, October 1718

'Fall back in line! Hoist the colours!'

'They're coming!'

As the crew scrambled to their positions, Dyer felt the adrenaline surge through his veins, electrifying his senses. The deck of *The Duchess* resonated with the rhythmic pounding of footsteps and the creaking of ropes.

Dyer had a feeling this moment would come. Morgan's father, Captain Craven, had long sought to bring her back into his fold, to bend her will to his own. This battle was long overdue. It was inevitable. Each member of the crew moved with grim faces as they readied themselves for the battle with the approaching enemy. Only the clash of steel would settle the score between them.

Just as Dyer was about to join the fray, a hand landed gently on his arm, sending tingles down his arm. 'Hey,' he heard the voice of Morgan. 'Be careful.'

Dyer turned towards his captain with a grin. She had a stoic look on her face that revealed nothing, and yet he could see that worry in her eyes. He cupped her face with his hands. 'Always, Ma'am.'

He leaned in to give her a kiss. It was short, but still took his breath away. 'I love you,' he professed once he pulled back.

'I know you do.' Morgan's cheeks looked flushed, and he could not deny she looked adorable.

'One day, I will get those words out of your pretty mouth.'

'I thought we settled this five months ago when I married you. Was that not enough?'

'It'll never be enough.' Dyer gave her one last kiss before heading to the bow.

The first volleys of cannon boomed, sending plumes of smoke billowing into the air as fiery projectiles streaked across the water. The two ships collided with a bone-jarring impact, the sound of splintering wood and twisting metal drowning out the cries of the crew.

Morgan stood tall at the helm; her expression steely as she barked orders to her crew. Despite the danger that surrounded her, her gaze was fierce; a determination to see her ship through the storm and emerge victorious on the other side. Dyer was at the forefront of the fray, his sword parried blow after blow. The deck beneath his feet was slick with blood and sweat. Flames licked at the sails.

Amidst the clash of swords and the roar of cannon fire, he spotted a hulking figure, its presence commanding respect. Dyer's stomach twisted as Craven squared off against Morgan. Their swords clashed with deadly precision. Despite Morgan's skill, Craven was the superior opponent; every strike was calculated. Without a second thought, Dyer sprang into action. His sword cut a path through the chaos towards his wife's side. Unable to reach her in time as Craven's blade struck true. With a cry of pain, Morgan staggered back, blood staining her clothes as she fought to stay on her feet.

Dyer threw himself between them, his own sword raised in a desperate bid to protect her from further harm. As he faced down Craven, his heart pounded in his chest, his every instinct screaming at him to fight on, no matter the cost.

And the cost was high.

'—Dyer, born on the fifteenth of February 1694, aged four-and-twenty.'

'Frederick Lewis, born on the seventh of September 1697, aged one-and-twenty.'

'We have come to collect you.'

A piercing scream cut through the air, wrenching Dyer from his thoughts with a jolt. It was a sound he had never heard before, and yet he recognised it in an instant. He turned his head, only to find her kneeling beside his lifeless body, her hands trembling as she reached out to touch his face, her tears mingling with the blood that stained his pale skin. And he was staring right through it.

'No...' Dyer felt his eyes burn with tears. His chest constricted with a pain unlike anything he had ever known. Was this it? Was this all the life he lived with her?

No, it cannot be.

He needed more time.

He wanted more time.

But the truth was more than clear. He was dead. He could not go back in time. He could only hear his wife sobbing his name, caring nothing for the battle unfurling around her.

Realisation hit him like a blow to the chest. The battle. The battle raged on around them, the clash of steel and the roar of cannons filling the air. People kept fighting for their death. She needed to focus, to fight for her life or she would die, too. And that was when he did not care about his pain anymore. He did not give a damn that he was dead.

He could go to Hell after this and not even care.

He needed her to live.

'Morgan!' He took long strides towards her. 'Morgan, snap out of it!'

Dyer crossed the distance between them, his heart pounding in his chest as he reached out to grab her by the arm. But to his horror, his hand passed right through her, as insubstantial as smoke. Frustration boiled within him as he made another futile attempt to reach her, his movements frantic. 'Damn it! Morgan!'

'She will be fine,' a calm voice echoed behind him.

Dyer turned, and that was when he saw the only two pairs of eyes that were able to see him. A woman and a man, both cloaked in black. There was nothing remarkable about them, only the piercing silver eyes of the man, who was staring with a blank face at him. Both were completely unemotional, as if they had seen this hundreds of times.

'What?' Dyer did not know what else he could say.

'Your wife will be fine. Her lifespan has been increased,' the woman informed.

'Unexpectedly, it seems,' the man added as he extended his hand to show Dyer an object.

It was a beautiful and intricate device, one that Dyer would not be able to possess, even in his wildest dreams. An hourglass made of the purest gold. It shone more than any treasure that he had encountered. The first peculiarity was Morgan's name engraved on it. The second was that the sand was floating towards the top half. It went against the laws of gravity. Like sorcery.

'What is that?'

'It's a life clock,' the woman replied. 'It's meant to calculate how many years a soul gets to live. We were assigned to collect her soul but…'

'This happened instead,' the man finished and took some steps until he placed the hourglass in Dyer's hand. He received a glare from his partner, as if what he had done was a forbidden act. But a shake of his head quieted her down.

The woman let out a sigh and turned to Dyer. 'Careful. You are holding her life in your hands. Break it, and she is done for.'

With dread and admiration, Dyer realised he was holding something precious. Her heart. No, it was more. It was as if he was holding a part of her soul, and he would not be surprised if that was true. It was pulsing with life, and the next thing he knew, his worries were thrown overboard. He felt nothing but relief.

'You saved her,' the man stated. 'And now she has more years to live.'

'That's more than alright. I'm at peace with it.' His words were not a lie. He was glad that he had died in her place. He had no regrets. He would do it again.

'Reaper Hugh,' Dyer heard the woman speak again.

'Yes, Reaper Ruby.'

'Return to the academy and retrieve Mr Dyer's hourglass for full extraction. Take Mr Lewis with you as well.'

'Wait, Lewis?' Dyer looked up from Morgan's hourglass. And there he was, his best friend, standing next to that woman. He had not acknowledged his presence until now. 'Lewis, what the hell…?'

He strode forward towards his friend, uncaring about the cloaked man's panicked face when he carried the hourglass away from his sight.

'Get that hourglass, Reaper Hugh!'

He paid no heed to Ruby. He stood in front of his friend. 'Lewis, you alright?'

'It all happened so fast.' Lewis shook his head. His shirt was covered in blood, and his eyes were bloodshot. He looked young, so young.

No one should have died this way.

'It all happened so fast, mate, I don't…' Lewis choked on his own saliva. 'I don't even know what hit me.'

'Hey, it's alright,' Dyer grabbed his friend by the shoulder with his free hand. 'It's all good now.'

'Mr Dyer,' Reaper Hugh approached him and extended his hand. 'The hourglass, please.'

'I…' Dyer looked down at the hourglass. Something so precious. He wanted to keep it forever. He felt tears prickle his eyes. He could still hear her screams; she was calling out for him. But when he looked up to search for his wife, the surrounding scenery had changed. They were still on the ship, but it was blurry. A mist was covering everything around them. It looked deserted, and yet there were faded silhouettes passing by. That was when the truth settled in once more. He was dead and stuck in this plane. 'What are you going to do with it?'

Hugh's silver eyes softened. 'Safeguard it. Until her new time passes.'

'Can I stay… until she passes away?' Dyer did not want her to die alone.

'You cannot. You are not allowed to stay on this plane for too long. You must cross, your soul must be judged.'

'Then why are you here? There must be a way, isn't that right?' He sounded desperate but did not care. If there was a way, he would take it.

'I suppose…' Reaper Hugh glanced at the woman in thought. 'Yes, you could do that.'

'Do what?'

'Work with us,' Reaper Hugh said, and when Reaper Ruby made a sound of protest, he held up his hand to continue. 'I do not think the Head would be opposed to it. After all, such a rare case, this one. An exception for an exception.'

'An exception?'

At that, Reaper Ruby let out a scoff. But Reaper Hugh's look made her relent. 'Not everyone sacrifices their life for another. It's a spur of the moment. Something that the Fates cannot predict. The very action that proves that the Fates do not control humanity in its entirety and that they, well, *you*, have free will to do as you choose. That millisecond where you choose to save a life cannot be counted in the hourglasses. Therefore, these rare occasions occur, where we are assigned to collect a soul but encounter another.

'And rare cases like this are offered… a boon… since the extraction is done differently from the protocol. So, only since you asked, we will offer this once. Become a reaper and help us guide souls to the Afterlife.'

Dyer let down an exhale. There was too much to process; his death, the fact that Morgan will remain alone, the existence of reapers and the possibility of remaining on this plane for longer. 'Will I be able to see her then?'

'If you are assigned to her, yes,' Reaper Hugh held up his finger in warning. 'No, we cannot guarantee that. Question is, are you willing to take the chance?'

'Always,' Dyer declared. Even if the possibility was minimal, he would do it. For her.

'Very well, we shall accommodate you for individual trials. That way, you will not have to wait until the end of the century.'

'Wait,' Lewis called out. 'What about me?'

Reaper Hugh turned to Lewis. 'Not you, I'm afraid. You were meant to die here, right in this moment. And you were not chosen during the Blood Moon. We cannot make exceptions for you. Your soul will be judged accordingly and be set for reincarnation when the appropriate time comes.'

'But...' Lewis began.

'It's alright,' Dyer said soothingly as he walked toward his friend. 'Reincarnation doesn't sound so bad, does it?'

Lewis gulped. 'I...'

Dyer tapped on his shoulder. 'You did good. You don't need to follow me everywhere. This is what was destined for me, and you should go where you belong. And who knows? Maybe our paths will cross again.'

Lewis nodded, his eyes averted to the ground. 'Aye, I hope so.'

Dyer gave his friend one last hug.

'See you on the other side, jackass,' Lewis mumbled, which earned him a laugh from Dyer.

That was how these friends departed.

Lewis made it to the Aboveworld, a realm where only the saints reside.

As for Dyer, he endured the trials set for him, later on becoming a reaper. But when Dyer could finally meet his lover again, he wanted desperately to erase what he had been forced to witness from his mind and wished he had left for the Afterlife after all.

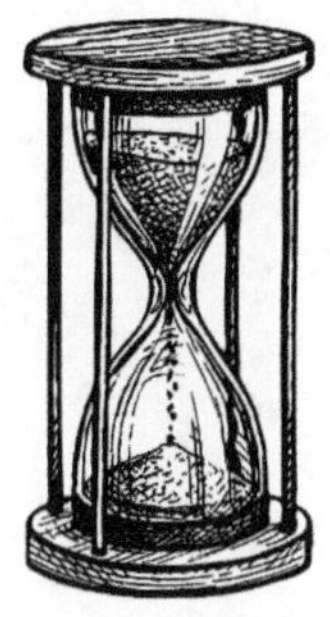

DISPUTE

'Emma Jenkins, born on the eighth of March 1990, aged thirty-five. We've come to collect you.'

The voice cut through the sunlight streamed room. Standing in the doorway was a tall figure shrouded by a haze of cigarette smoke. His most striking feature, however, were his eyes; silver orbs that shimmered with an ethereal glow.

'W-what the...' Emma's voice wavered. 'How do you know my name?'

'I'm here to escort you,' the man replied, his expression unreadable as he regarded Emma with an intensity that sent shivers down her spine.

'Escort? Where?'

'To the Afterlife.'

'Huh?' She questioned again in complete disbelief. She shook her head in denial, as if the entire situation were a hallucination. Her feet were glued to the ground. The mere presence of the man standing before her was pulling her away from reality. She tried to recall the last thing she did before waking up. Her life had not been that remarkable. Flashes of memories flickered in her mind; her morning routine, a tube ride to work, a dinner with college friends, another journey back home and then nothing. She must have been in an accident, she realised, her thoughts spiralling. But how could this be real?

'Look,' he motioned with his head to the front, right at the couch.

A figure lay motionless, bathed in the soft light of the afternoon sun. The corpse mocked Emma with its stillness.

'What... what happened?' Her voice quivered as she took in the sight before her.

'You were dumb. That's what,' The figure retorted, a sneer curling his lip. He put out his cigarette with the sole of his shoe and threw it to her couch. 'There was gas leaking out of your stove, and you didn't notice.'

'Theo, don't be like that,' a female voice admonished.

'What, it's true, innit?' Theo's response was unapologetic, his gaze fixing on his partner.

'It sounds completely unprofessional if I have to be frank.' The young woman pinched the bridge of her nose. 'Points can be deducted.'

'And who's gonna tell?' Theo pointed at Emma. 'Her? I don't think so.'

'There might be eyes everywhere.'

'You are getting paranoid, Becca, and I don't like it.'

'Look, let's…'

Emma tuned out after that. Their conversation almost muted as she stared at her own corpse.

She couldn't believe it. This was it? Was she supposed to accept that her life was over? Her thoughts spiralled into a frantic inventory of all the things she hadn't done, each one a sharp pang of regret.

She regretted not having the time to travel more. She had flown to New York for a corporate meeting, spent her evenings in posh hotel lounges rather than exploring Central Park or the museums. She had attended a tech summit in San Francisco but hadn't bothered to walk through the Golden Gate Bridge or take a stroll through Haight-Ashbury. During a business trip to Rome, she had spent her free hours networking at high-end restaurants instead of visiting the Colosseum or the Vatican. In Sydney, she had sipped cocktails with clients at a rooftop bar but hadn't set foot on the iconic Sydney Opera House steps or walking along Bondi Beach. Even a trip to Tokyo, which had been filled with luxurious dinners and meetings in gleaming skyscrapers, had left her without a single visit to the temples or the street markets.

She had a stable job as marketing director but knew she had bigger ambitions. She wanted to write, to create stories that would captivate and inspire others. The unfinished manuscripts on her computer now felt like monuments to her unrealised potential.

Each of these missed opportunities were now distant fantasies, slipping through her fingers.

She regretted not finding true love. She had dated here and there, but her heart hadn't found its other half. The thought of having never experienced the deep connection and passion she had read about in her beloved romance novels was almost unbearable. She wouldn't have the chance to share her life with someone, to build a future together, to feel the warmth of a partner by her side.

Family weighed heavily on her mind. She had distanced herself from her parents and siblings, assuming there would be time to mend those relationships, to bridge the gaps that had formed over the years. She envisioned visits home and casual conversations that were out of reach.

She was even going to miss the simple pleasures of life, the small things she had taken for granted. The taste of her favourite coffee, the feeling of the sun on her face during a morning walk, the cosy evenings spent reading by the window.

All these moments felt like lost treasures.

'Apologies, Miss Jenkins,' she heard her name once

more from the young woman and her face turned in her direction. 'It's time.'

'T-time?' Emma quaked. 'No, this can't be happening. I'm not ready to go. I have so much I haven't done. I'm not ready to die.'

'I know,' Becca sympathised. 'Everyone feels that way. But your time is up. You can't go back to your body. You must cross to the Afterlife.'

Her eyes filled with tears, blurring the figure of the man before her. She wanted to shout, to scream at the unfairness of it all. Her heart pounded in her chest; each beat a frantic plea for more time. She wasn't ready to leave this world, to let go of her dreams, her hopes, her life.

But as she stood there, rooted to the spot, she felt an overwhelming force pulling her toward the inevitable. The man, Theo, extended his hand, revealing an hourglass. She could feel the pull of its presence.

And the world blurred in her eyes.

'What's your bet?'

'Netherworld, obviously.'

The sky had deepened into a velvety indigo, and the city was bathed in the muted glow of street lamps. Near

Canary Wharf, the area was a blend of sleek, modern apartment buildings and the stoic remnants of historic warehouses. This side of London was quieter than other areas, and car horns were replaced with the rhythmic clinking of cyclists' bells.

Becca frowned, her brow furrowing as she considered his words. 'She didn't do anything notorious…'

Theo let out a sharp laugh. 'She was a bitch, that's what. A conceited girl who was never thankful nor bothered to appreciate. She never apologised and felt the rest of the world were her minions.'

Becca turned her gaze to the cobblestones, her expression thoughtful. 'You really think that's enough to send her to the Netherworld?'

Her partner nodded, his expression hardening. 'And you know what's worse? She didn't even acknowledge it. She thought everything that she was doing was right. No self-awareness, no humility. Just pure, unadulterated arrogance.'

The path ahead curved, leading them closer to the water's edge. The soft lapping of the Thames against the dock created a soothing rhythm in the quiet evening. They approached a small, secluded spot where the river's edge met a wooden pier, a perfect place to step into a water portal.

'Maybe.' Becca sighed. 'But sometimes people are more complex than we give them credit for.'

'Perhaps.' Theo shrugged. 'But in the end, it's not our call to make. We just deliver the souls and let the higherups sort it out.'

Just as they were about to step into the shimmering water portal, a voice rang out. *'Ey, ey, stop!'*

Becca turned around, her brow furrowing. 'What?' She scanned the surroundings, her eyes settling on two figures approaching at warp speed.

The newcomers were unfamiliar to them, but their dark robes and the aura of command they exuded marked them as fellow reapers. Judging by their leathered corsets and bracers, it was clear they had not been selected in the twentieth century pool. The woman with a piercing silvery gaze spoke first. 'What on earth are you doing?'

'Uh, is this part of…?' Becca trailed off as she exchanged a glance with Theo.

Theo, equally baffled, stepped forward. 'How should I know? Um, who are you?'

'The question is, who are you? That's our soul,' the second newcomer, a stern-looking woman with intense blue eyes, talked next.

Becca's eyes widened, her grip on the strap of her chain sickle tightening. 'Excuse us?'

Without warning, the duo's saint vanished, materialising directly in front of Theo. 'Give it here'.

'Uh, Becca?' Theo glanced in alarm at his partner.

Becca, sensing the tension, tapped his shoulder and materialised them a few feet away from the strangers.

'No, thank you.' Theo snapped his fingers, causing the saint to freeze in place, her expression locked in a mask of irritation. 'Ha! Sucks to be you.'

'That's against protocol!' the sinner warned. 'You can get detained for this.'

'Whoa, chill, girl. She's unharmed.' Theo rolled his eyes.

'Didn't you read the Codex? Attacking another reaper is forbidden and can be punishable.'

'Fine! Jeez.' Theo snapped his fingers once more, releasing her partner from his grip.

'Listen, folks,' the saint growled, taking steps towards them. 'We were not asking. We're telling. Give us the hourglass. That soul belongs to Argentina.'

'Where's that? Africa?'

'*Es joda? No sabe geografí*a? It's South America,' the saint's shoulders tensed, anticipating their next question. 'And no, it does not belong to Mexico.'

Becca dragged Theo a couple of steps back with her arm with a glare. It was clear that he was not helping. 'Forgive him. He lacks manners sometimes. I'm Becca. And that's my partner, Theo. Can you tell us what's going on?'

'That soul is of Latin American descent. That means she belongs to our jurisdiction,' the saint gritted her teeth.

'Her name is not Spanish, you dowager.' Theo scoffed. 'Emma *Sofía* Jenkins.'

Theo waved his hand, dismissing them. 'That... doesn't say anything to me. Also, she's white.'

'The fuck?' The saint's temper flared, her eyes narrowing. 'Latin Americans are not white.'

'No, no, let's not go there, Theo,' Becca cautioned, placing a hand on his arm.

'*Ah, este es un imbécil importante,*' the saint muttered under her breath, shaking her head.

Theo's eyes squinted, as if that would help him understand the language. 'Did you just call me an imbecile?'

'Oh, so you are a tiny bit smart. I was wondering how you got chosen,' she drawled.

The sinner stepped between them. 'Now, now, no one here is going to talk about race, skin tone, whatever. This is a matter of where the soul belongs.'

'Well, we're not just going to hand it over. We'll fail the exam,' Theo's grip tightened on the hourglass. There was no way he would give it up.

The blue eyed sighed. It was clear to them she was frustrated. But so were they. 'Ugh... don't tell me.'

'You're in the second-phase trial?' the other woman asked, a hint of understanding in her voice.

'Yeah, so?' Theo lifted his chin up.

'And no one bothered to check if there might be some jurisdictional issues with the soul?'

'Uh, maybe because there are no jurisdictional issues in the first place?'

'Let's just take a breather, alright? Call your superior.'

'There's no way. We'll fail,' Theo's jaw set.

'I'll do it.'

Theo's eyes widened and turned to her partner. 'Becca! Are you bloody serious?'

'I don't think we'll lose points for reporting a problem. Making an unauthorised decision is worse,' she reasoned as she reached for her cellphone.

It didn't take long for their mentor to appear. Within moments, the water portal by the river expanded, and he stepped through, his tall frame and flowing dark coat giving him an imposing presence. 'I'm Master Reaper James. I oversee the training of the newbies this year.'

The girl group exchanged a quick glance before stepping forward. 'Master Reaper,' The sinner nodded in acknowledgement. 'I'm Reaper Luisa. My partner's Reaper Daniela.' The saint inclined her head in a respectful bow, her earlier irritation replaced by a formal demeanour.

James observed the Argentinian reapers, his eyes lingering on them for a moment before shifting to his mentees. Becca and Theo stood a little straighter, pretending to be professionals.

'Master James,' Theo greeted, just as Becca gave her superior a formal nod.

'You're not in trouble,' James reassured them. 'You won't fail either. You have fulfilled the marking criteria.'

'Thank you, Master James.' Becca let out a sigh.

Theo, still holding the hourglass, looked between James and the strangers. 'But, sir, they said the soul belongs to their jurisdiction.'

James turned his gaze back to the foreigners. 'There seems to be a misunderstanding. It seems Emma Sofía Jenkins, despite her descent, falls under a unique category. Our records show she was born in Argentina but lived her entire life in Europe. An oversight on our part, yes. But the soul still belongs to us.'

Was this his way of telling them he didn't give a shit?

Daniela's frown deepened, and she crossed her arms over her chest. 'Article Seven, Section Three of the Codex states that jurisdiction is determined by the soul's place of residence at the time of birth. She lived in Argentina, which makes her our responsibility.'

James met her gaze. 'That is true, Reaper Daniela, but Section Five, Addendum C clearly outlines exceptions for souls with significant ties to a region. In this case, it is the United Kingdom.'

Luisa's eyes narrowed. 'Section Nine, Addendum B specifies that in cases of dispute, the soul must be returned to the place of death of her ancestors for final rites. We have the authority here.'

James's expression remained calm. 'But Article Eleven, Section Two allows for a temporary hold on the soul until a council review can determine the proper jurisdiction. This is not just a matter of place of ancestry; it involves the place where she chose to live and where she died.'

Daniela's nostrils flared. 'We have our own protocol for these situations, James. Apologies, *Master Reaper* James. We cannot just hand over the soul because of some training exercise. It's our duty to ensure she is guided correctly.'

James stepped forward, his gaze darkening. 'And it is our duty to ensure that the Codex is followed to the letter. This soul represents more than just a point in a trial. It's about respecting the path this particular soul walked.'

Theo, watching the exchange with wide eyes, whispered to Becca, 'Are we going to get into trouble for this?'

'No. He even said we did the right thing by calling him. This is beyond our scope.' Becca shook her head and look at her feet. A frown formed on her face, noting the changing light. 'Wait, hold on a sec.'

Becca's head turned to look at the horizon. *Fuck.* 'Guys…' Becca began, but the others were too engrossed in their debate to notice. She turned to face the group as Luisa began to attempt mediating.

'We can contact the High Council for a rapid decision. There's no need to escalate this further.'

'That's precisely what I intend to do,' James crossed his arms. 'If I have to cite the entire Codex to the Council, that's exactly what I'll do. Her permanent residency in England, for exam—'

'Guys!' Becca shouted louder.

'Ow! Something pinched me!' Theo jumped back, almost dropping the hourglass.

'Theo, what's going on?' Becca's hand tried to reach him.

The hourglass in Theo's hand cracked, a web of fractures spreading across its surface. He dropped the artefact to the floor as if it were boiling water. A thick mist began to rise from the sand, swirling around them. The mist cleared, revealing Emma, her eyes completely black, a sinister grin forming on her face. Becca's heart dropped to her stomach and sprinted back, dragging Theo with her by the arm.

'Black hand!' Luisa warned and summoned her chain sickle from the nothingness.

'Newbies, stand back,' James ordered, his voice steady. He summoned his chain sickle from the ground, out of nothingness. The blade gleamed in the fading light, with a golden otherworldly glow.

Emma's form twisted, her grin widening. Theo and Becca obeyed their mentor and took a few more steps back, perhaps way more than necessary. The training exercises had not prepared them for something like this, and they were not going to risk it.

Not for the ones who screwed this up for them.

James swung his chain sickle, the blade arcing through the air toward Emma, who let out a haunting laugh. 'You think you can contain me again?' she hissed, her voice echoing in an unnatural way.

James's eyes narrowed. 'We will send you to your proper place, spirit. You cannot defy the natural order.'

Emma lunged forward, her spectral form moving with unnerving speed. James met her attack head on, his chain sickle slashing through the air with a crackle of energy. The blade connected with Emma's form, but she recoiled, her grin not faltering. Her black hands swiping through the air with lethal intent.

Luisa and Daniela moved in synchrony, circling Emma from either side. Luisa's chain sickle lashed out, wrapping around Emma's arm and pulling taut. Daniela took the opportunity to strike, her sickle aiming for Emma's exposed side. Emma screeched, her form flickering as she struggled against the chains binding her.

With a fluid motion, James spun his sickle, the chain extending and wrapping around Emma's arm. He yanked hard, pulling her off balance. Luisa seized the opportunity, her sickle cutting through Emma's side, eliciting a piercing scream.

Emma retaliated, her spectral hand shooting out and grabbing Daniela by the throat. The saint gasped, struggling as dark tendrils of energy seeped into her skin. James stepped forward, his sickle slashing down and severing Emma's grip, freeing Daniela.

Emma shrieked, the blackness in her eyes expanding, her form becoming more monstrous. She struck with her other hand, hurling dark energy at the reapers. James raised his sickle, absorbing the impact with a light shield.

'Hold your ground!' James commanded.

The reapers circled Emma, their chain sickles creating tendrils of light. Emma's form flickered, her energy waning. James struck, his blade crossing through Emma's chest. She let out an ear-splitting scream, and her form disintegrated into a cloud of dark mist.

'Oh, gods, that was scary,' Becca breathed out, her fingers trembling as she released her hold on Theo's jacket.

'Well, that was one hell of a ghost story.'

Becca rolled her eyes. 'Theo, really?'

'Alright, you two.' James dropped the chain sickle to the ground, the weapon disappearing from sight with a faint shimmer. 'Good work. Get rest and write up a full report on this incident.'

Theo groaned. 'Seriously? Homework?'

'Let's just get it done,' Becca patted on Theo's arm.

'Fine, how do you spell "spectacularly horrifying"?'

'Mr Davies,' James butted in, arching an eyebrow. 'Perhaps you should reconsider your choice of company. Miss Henley's influence seems to be rubbing off on you.'

'I believe Theo is the bad influence, not our poor friend.'

'Hey, I thought you were on my side, Becca,' he protested, feigning innocence. He glanced at the Argentinian reapers. 'Great meeting you, girls. Let's not do this ever again.'

'Agreed,' Luisa let out a soft smile.

'It's been… interesting,' Daniela let out with a strained voice, before staggering, clutching her throat. Her face contorted in pain, and a dark, smoky tendril seeped from her mouth, curling like a living shadow.

'Daniela!' Luisa cried, rushing to her partner's side.

James stamped forward. 'Step back,' he ordered, his voice hard. Becca and Theo's hearts pounded as their mentor extended a hand, a faint glow emanating from his palm. Nothing happened. The dark tendril resisted, thrashing with force. In that spur of a moment, the younglings realised they stumbled upon something far more sinister than they could handle.

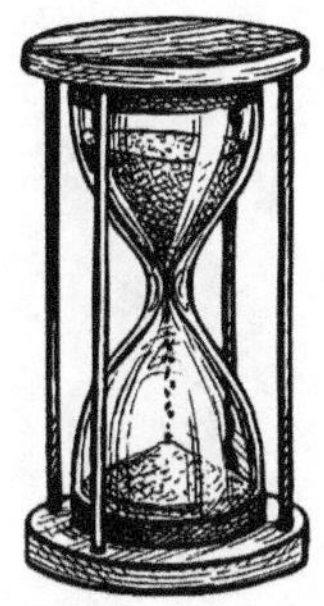

RECOLLECTION

Reaper Grace had no one she wished to see again. Her colleagues did not want to hang out and preferred roam around their relatives. Grace would have done the same, truth be told.

If she remembered anyone who missed her.

What kind of freedom were sinners provided with after passing the Moon Trial? Some peace and relief that she would not be turned to dust? She was forced to witness a newbie die not so long ago for not being good enough. For being different. She felt different too, and that scared her to no end, no matter how hard she pretended. Today was the day she had to get away from that frigid place, from those endless hallways, from the smell of those flowers. From the academy.

After getting the approval, she didn't know what to do with her time, so she started small. A perk to being a ghost is that they didn't have to pay those unreasonable transit fares. £3.40 a single ride to central was ridiculous to her. Grace got in the first Jubilee train she saw and, the next thing she knew, her feet dragged her to the Overground line. She could breathe despite the suffocating air inside the coach. No one could touch her, anyway. No one could see her. No one could hear her. She sat on the floor next to the sliding doors and waited.

The journey seemed to never end, but her body did not let Grace stand until she reached Wapping. She walked up the pebbled damp stairs and out of the station. There wasn't much to see in this neighbourhood, only a stoned path of warehouses made of beige bricks. Every now and then, there were narrow alleys she could turn down. She took one of the alleys and walked down some steep stairs that led her to a rocky pier. There was no one here. She could only hear the river colliding with the pebbles and the seagulls screeching. Her hands were cold. She thought reapers did not have such sensations. At one point, her legs no longer wanted to move. She forced herself out of that paralysis to walk along the path beside the river. The water was duller than the blue of her hair. She had seen better.

Wait, had she?

Turning her attention towards the lonely gallows, her steps led her closer to the imposing structure. The wooden framework stood weathered and worn. Its stark silhouette contrasted against the soft colours of the evening sky, a sombre reminder of the grim purpose it once served. As she reached out to touch the rough-hewn wood, she could feel the echoes of lives lost and injustice served. Traces of rusted chains dangled from its beams. So many souls met their end here.

Stories untold.

Voices silenced.

Their corpses were burned and buried in the ground, in a desperate attempt to have them erased from people's minds.

A flutter stirred in her chest as she wondered about the tales hidden within these timbers, and a steady warmth settled in her core, driving her to remember those who came before. She wanted to know why she had this unnecessary need to feel connected to a past that might not have belonged to her. It struck her how cruel people were, indifferent to the countless souls who once stood in this same spot, facing their fate with bravery, fear or resignation. Grace took a last glance at the river, its surface now tinged with the hues of twilight, before turning away without looking back.

'I can't believe you're here.'

Grace didn't need to look at the source of the voice to see who was behind her. She could recognise that tone anywhere. Remembering her mentor didn't seem to be a problem, unlike every other memory she wasn't allowed to retain. Maybe it was true that an empty head meant more room for knowledge. Deadly knowledge.

Master Reaper James sat next to her on the wooden bench. She had found this pub not far from the piers. The outdoor tables led straight to a pleasant view of the Thames. Unlike mortals, she could gaze right through the darkness like a cat, able to discern the river from the sky. Her silver eyes shone despite the lack of light around them.

'How did you know where I was?'

'We have to keep track of all reapers who wander around. Is that beer?' James pointed at her pint.

'Cider. I don't like beer.' She frowned, staring at the golden liquid. 'I think.'

Grace hadn't been able to talk to the bartender but could sneak into the bar and pour herself a drink. She held out the glass to him. 'Want some?'

James hesitated for a moment and then snatched the glass from her to take a long swig.

'Hey!' Grace stopped him.

'Don't want people to think you're drunk when you get back to the academy.' James handed her back the pint.

'I didn't know you could get drunk out of one pint.'

'I've met weak people before. Not fun to hang out with them.'

Grace turned to look at James. 'Wait, can reapers get drunk?'

'Obviously.'

'Then, I must have a high metabolism,' she observed, glad for it. She didn't want to risk embarrassing herself in front of people she barely knew. 'Besides, if I wanted to get drunk, I would've picked something stronger.'

'Huh. What's your poison? Vodka?'

'Rum.'

James paused and turned his sight to the river with a pensive look. At first, Grace thought he didn't like her answer, but maybe that was just her imagination.

'Funny,' he decided.

'Why?'

James shrugged. 'Just saying. Not the usual drink of choice of young women.'

'That's sexist.' She crinkled her nose.

'That's a fact. Also, have you even drunk rum lately to be able to say that? Snuck into my cabinet perhaps?'

'You keep it unlocked?'

'Not anymore.'

'You're no fun.' Grace's corner lip turned upwards as she went back to sip on her pint, aiming to finish it.

James grabbed the hand that held the glass and lower it. An unfamiliar tingle ran through her skin, her fingers suddenly warmer.

Grace scoffed and turned to James. 'I told you I—'

'We have work to do.'

Gods, no. She travelled far for a *reason.*

James slipped out an element from his pocket. A golden orienteering compass needle. He handed it to her, and she stared at it. The needle levitated a few centimetres away from her hand. Specks of golden dust fell from the needle and into her hand from time to time, which would later disappear. The needle moved, pointing northeast.

'A case? With *you*? What an honour,' Grace mused, and James saw right into her bullshit.

'Focus. Her name is Clare Richards, aged three-and-seventy. Cause of death, stroke.'

Grace's gaze focused on the compass. The needle shone at the mention of the mortal's name. It was calling out for her. 'Was it caused by an accident or…?'

'It was just her way to go.'

Grace noted how clinical James was about death. How many cases did he get assigned until he had no choice but to get used to it? How many years did it take him until he felt nothing for the souls he had to reap? It was like when doctors needed to operate. How many bodies did they need to see until they separated their feelings from it? That begged the question, how long would it take her until she was completely detached?

She took a quick glance at James, noticing how weary his onyx eyes were. Reapers had no need to sleep unless they wished to. No need to indulge in the little things of life unless they wanted to be selfish for a while. But she had a feeling he needed some sort of rest, as if the number of centuries he had been reaping souls demanded him to take a break from responsibilities. And that was the only thing that stopped a complaint from coming out of her mouth. Grace had no wish to work tonight; she was even promised a day off. But it seemed death took no breaks.

The sand tingled in her hand right before it disappeared. 'Why does it do that?'

'What?'

'The sand.'

'Oh, it's the life of the future dead soul.'

Grace had never held a cockroach before, but this might be probably the closest feeling to it. Perhaps James saw the mortified look on her face, as he let out a hoarse laugh.

'Uh, no. Not like that. It's the—' he trailed off as if trying to find the right words. 'Essence of the soul. The part that clings to the living. The compass captures that to pinpoint its location. Nothing gory, I promise. Even I cannot fully grasp the extent of what it really means.'

'Oh,' she let out, still staring at the sandy artefact.

'That's all you're going to say?'

'Uh, yes?' She frowned. What else was there to say?

'Then can you stop making that face?'

Any other reaper would have judged Grace for taking the train to Whitechapel instead of using the water portals, but James did not seem to mind. At least at first.

They were sitting in one of the last coaches, enjoying the silence. Grace came to realise he could tell how nervous she was about this, as he stared at the way she was twiddling her thumbs. He knew, and that was why he let her drag this on as long as possible. She hated it. She hated how he could see right through her, even though she tried her hardest to hide it. Was he taking pity on her?

'You could have said no,' Grace spoke up after the doors closed. She had noticed he was staring hard at the mortals that were sitting near them. They were not doing anything notorious, just staring at their phones, with the occasional typing or scrolling movement. But he looked like he didn't want to be here at all.

'There's still time until Richards's death. I don't mind taking the long way.'

'You are very patient,' Grace noted, and that made James turn his head to look at her. 'For being a relic.'

'Are you calling me old?'

'I heard you were around three centuries old.'

'Does that bother you?'

Grace shook her head. 'Aren't you bored? Of this? You don't seem to like people. At least not these newest generations.'

'That gives me more incentive to judge them.'

At that, Grace wanted to laugh. 'So, no reincarnation plans for the future?'

'That door will always be open for me, whether I want it or not,' James sighed, leaning on his back against the seat. 'Boss placed that on the table for me multiple times.'

'But you declined.'

'Do you know why reapers work so hard? It's not because they have no choice.'

'I thought it was because we're threatened to be sent to the Netherworld,' Grace drawled. She felt she was trying too hard to pretend that she did not feel threatened. A task that was almost impossible, since failing was never an option.

Failure sent new recruits to a place worse than the Netherworld. They called it Oblivion, the stage where a soul would vanish from all corners of the Earth, unable to reincarnate. Failures were turned into nothing. And so, missions like this had to go right. She just hoped that her skills were up to par.

'That might work for new recruits like you,' James chuckled. 'But after a hundred years or so the incentive is another. The more you work, the higher the golden spoon you receive when you reincarnate.'

'You become richer in your next life?' Grace frowned. It sounded petty to her, shallow even. But she was not going to say that in front of her instructor.

'It's anything you wish for. Fortune, fame, good health, a stable family. You can have a go with the Fates and decide what your new thread looks like. It's not something that you want to miss. And the more years you give to the company of immortals, the more choices you get to make once you're in that Destiny Room.

'Things like money, "being the son of", contacts or even this shit called being an influencer doesn't work here. We believe in a meritocracy; the harder you work, the higher the reward. And how sweet the reward is once you do things the right way,' James finished.

Grace nodded and looked out the window, watching the people dispersing as they got off the train. One more stop to go. She didn't know if he was selling the job to her or if that was his true opinion. But if this plane worked that way…

'And you?' Grace inquired. 'How long are you planning to wait before you quit being a reaper?'

'I'm not leaving this realm any time soon,' James tilted his head at her. 'Things here have become more interesting since your arrival.'

The compass needle led them down Court Street until they reached the entrance of the Royal London Hospital. They climbed the back stairs until the fourth floor.

The hallway smelled like lemon scented disinfectant and clinical antiseptic. Grace surveyed the unfamiliar room. The needle shone brighter, sensing how near the soul was to them. Yet Grace did not move an inch past reception. She looked down at her feet, shifting her weight between them, and waited for instructions. She was hoping James would tell her to wait outside.

She knew that would not happen.

'Alright, crash course,' James turned towards her. 'Do you know why reapers go in pairs?'

'Balance?'

'What kind of balance?'

'Between sinners and saints, I guess?' Grace frowned. 'Sinners have a new way to repent, not that I remember what I done—'

'Of power,' James corrected her. 'That's how our objects come to be. Yes, all reapers can manipulate hourglasses and crystals. But the creation of these elements relies solely on the type of reaper you are. Crystals represent the memories and emotions of a soul, something that saints still have intact. Whereas the sand represents the life of the soul as a whole. The hourglass is an objective element, useful until the moment it arrives to the Judgement Room. As objective as—'

'—the sinners,' Grace finished. 'Because we don't remember those things.'

'Good,' James handed Grace the hourglass that he had taken out from his coat.

Grace stared at the name engraved on the bottom of the hourglass.

Clare Richards

The sand was just about to run out from the top.

'What about the compass? Who creates it?'

'Oh, no, we only have one arrow, and it uses the same sand of the soul located in the hourglass. You'll get one after graduation.'

'How wonderful,' Grace grimaced did her best to ensure her tone was as less sarcastic as possible. 'Best. Gift. Ever.'

They found Clare in a private room, surrounded by the soft hum of machines and the steady beep of a heart monitor. A nurse was leaving the room, unaware of the two unseen visitors standing in the corner.

Clare's breath became more laboured, each rise and fall of her chest a struggle. The hourglass in Grace's hand mirrored the fleeting moments, the sand slipping away relentlessly.

James placed a comforting hand on her shoulder. 'Are you ready?'

Grace nodded, her grip tightening on the hourglass. 'Let's do this.' She braced herself for the inevitable moment when the last grain of sand would fall.

James approached Clare's bedside as he removed one of his gloves and extended his hand to her forehead. A sudden tremor rippled through Clare's body. At first, it was barely perceptible, a subtle quiver beneath her skin. But then, with alarming speed, the tremor escalated into a violent spasm, causing Clare to convulse. James recoiled, his hand pulling away from Clare's trembling form.

Grace's eyes widened, as she rushed to Clare's side. Her heart pounded as the old woman's body contort with pain. She reached out with trembling hands for the dying patient, but James's hand shot out, halting her in her tracks.

'Stay back.' His tone leaving no room for argument. 'If you can't do that, shut them down.'

'Shut down, what?'

'Your emotions. Sinners can temporarily suppress their emotions. You've done that during your Moon Trial without even knowing.'

Clare's condition deteriorated before her eyes. It was a cruel sight, one that Grace found herself powerless to stop. She could only watch, her fists clenched at her sides, feeling the raw edges of her emotions threatening to overwhelm her.

'How?'

'Picture a room in your mind and a ball of light where you would place all your emotions. Then see yourself walking out of that room and close the door.'

Taking a deep breath, Grace forced herself to focus inward. She pictured a heavy door closing in her heart, sealing away the tumultuous waves of sorrow and helplessness that threatened to consume her. Bit by bit, a numbness spread through her, until there was nothing.

The scene before her played out like a muted drama.

Nurses rushed to her aid, but there was nothing they could do. It was already done. The machines beside the bed emitted a soft beep, a solemn confirmation of her passing.

In this state of enforced serenity, Grace was aware of every detail; the sterile smell of the hospital room, the hushed murmurs of the medical staff, the cold light of the overhead lamps, but none of it touched her.

She was a spectator, removed from the anguish of the moment.

Beside the bed, Clare's soul materialised, a faint, shimmering silhouette that took on her features. She looked around with wide eyes and glanced down at her own body inert on the bed.

James stood in silence by the soul's side as Grace stepped forward. 'Clare Richards, born on the tenth of January 1952, aged seventy-three. We've come to collect you.'

'Is it time?' Clare's voice trembled.

Grace met her gaze. 'Yes, Clare. It's time.'

With a sense of quiet acceptance, Clare nodded.

The golden hourglass in her hand glowed brighter. Clare's body responded; her form disintegrated. Tiny particles of sand drifted away on an unseen breeze. Grace held the hourglass steady, in silence, as Clare's essence slipped away, each grain of sand a fragment of her being now contained within the confines of the artefact. And as the last remnants of her form disappeared, Grace closed her eyes, offering a silent prayer for Clare's journey beyond.

May she reincarnate in peace.

'It'll rain tomorrow.'

The air outside was cool and crisp, a stark contrast to the sterile confines of the building they had just left behind. She could hear the distant sounds of traffic, their footsteps echoing against the pavement as they walked out of the hospital grounds. The streetlights cast pools of golden light on the pavement, illuminating their path as they made their way down the steps and onto the street.

James turned to look at Grace. 'How do you know?'

'Oh,' Grace pointed at the starry sky, drawing a circle with her index finger. 'There's a halo around the moon. That usually means it'll rain.'

'That or we are in a country where it's more rainy than sunny.' A small smile tugged at James's his lips.

But that smile left as soon as it appeared. He fell silent for a moment, his eyes studying her. He stepped closer and his hand circled around her upper arm, the warmth of his hand seeping through the fabric of her jacket. In an instant, a soothing energy flowed over her, unravelling the mental barriers she had put up. Grace felt a rush of sensations flood back into her, the coldness in her heart melting away.

'Are you all right?' James hesitated to let go.

Grace shrugged, pulling her coat tighter around her shoulders with a shiver. Without a word, he took off his long black coat, the fabric whispering as it fell from his shoulders. He draped it over Grace's shoulders, the warmth of it enveloping her like a protective embrace.

Grace glanced up at him, her breath catching as she registered the gesture. For a moment, their eyes met, a silent understanding passing between them. With a grateful smile, she pulled the coat tighter around her as they resumed their walk, the scent of James's earthy cologne mingling with the night air.

'Good job today. Write a report and hand it to my desk tomorrow. I'll make sure Reaper Ruby gives you a few extra points for assisting last minute.'

Grace felt a tight knot form in her stomach as she listened to James's instructions. This was not the first time he had gone out of his way to help her, and while she appreciated his support, she couldn't shake the feeling that there was more to his actions than met the eye. Some would call it special treatment, but Grace couldn't help but wonder if James was trying too hard to ensure her position as a reaper.

'Mind if I ask you a question?'

'Go for it.'

'Why are you trying so hard to have me succeed?'

'If I didn't help my newbies succeed, that would make me a terrible mentor, don't you think?' James countered, crossing his arms. 'Believe me, my motives are not that pure nor altruistic.'

'So, you take all of your trainees to these unexpected-but-not-really death cases?' Sometimes it was hard to trust James's intentions. After all, they had not known each other for long. She just wished she could.

She assessed James's conflicted expression, and, after a defeated sigh, he relented. 'Because you were assigned to me. You are my soul. And I take care of all of my souls.'

And Grace wished she knew what on earth that meant.

Acknowledgements

They say writing a book is a lonely process, but I was never truly alone. I am extremely grateful for the lovely people who have accompanied me in every step of the way.

To my parents, Andrea and Marcelo, and my sister, Lucía. Thank you for your unwavering support and for reminding me I should pursue my dreams no matter what. And to my furry, fluffy Persian companions, Pepe and Santino, thank you for keeping me company as I crafted the first draft of this manuscript.

To my aunt and uncle, Vale and Enrique. Your constant guidance have been my North Star throughout this journey. I wouldn't be here without your wisdom.

To Agus and Ross T., for practically adopting me and helping me through tough and sleep-deprived times.

To Adam Baron, my writing course leader. Your insights on my story helped to shape this book into what it is today.

To Agus, because she deserves a whole paragraph for herself. Thank you for being there from the moment I sat at the café Le Blé with avocado toasts and enormous coffee mugs on our table and asked you, 'what if?'. Thank you for shaping the Overworld with me, giving me endless advice and for telling me it was okay to kill your boyfriend in one of my short stories. Thank you, Fede. I owe you a sandwich (and a gift bag).

To my school besties, Caro and Cande. Thank you for telling me it was okay to pursue my dreams elsewhere.

To my lovely uni friends, Delfi and Luli. Thank you for your endless encouragement and for listening to me rant about my writing ambitions.

To my beta readers, Ally and Annie. Thank you for your constructive critiques and encouragement. Your advice has been key in turning this book into something truly special.

To my Sparkletits – Alice, Holly, Yaz, Emma, Lina and Ruta. Thank you, thank you, thank you for being the most supportive and kind beings in the whole world. You brought many smiles to my face and filled my closet with fantasy outfits.

To my Thornback crew, Kara, Reyna and Vero. Thank you for being social with me in silence, drinking coffee almost every single day as we searched for balance between writing, job applications and apartment viewings.

To my ARC readers, thank you for sharing your enthusiasm for my book. It has been truly motivating.

To my Managing Editor, Julieta Pereyra. You are a star.

And lastly, to **you**, my readers. Your support, readership, messages and reviews mean the world to me, and I cannot thank you enough. This book is for you. I can't wait for you to join me on my next novel, following Grace Henley's and James Dyer's adventures in the Overworld.

Wait... have I confused you?

Stay tuned for more!

ABOUT THE AUTHOR

Jules Pendragon emerged from the shimmering mists, conjured by a legendary magician. Raised in the shifting rooms of the Moving Castle, she learned to weave spells into words. With a quill dipped in stardust, she crafts stories that transform the mundane world into extraordinary realms filled with mythical creatures. An elusive figure, Jules prefers the enchantment of anonymity and often hops into new lands, gathering inspiration from every corner. When not writing, she enjoys sipping coffee, concocting potions, befriending cats and exploring tales of dragons, grim reapers and mythological lore.

Instagram: @julespendragon_
TikTok: @julespendragon
Pinterest: @julespendragon_
Goodreads: @julespendragon
https://linktr.ee/julespendragon